序　言

　　自教育部實施「全民英檢」初級測驗以來，參加考試的人數逐年增加，顯示國人越來越重視這項檢定考試。我們的「初級英語聽力檢定①②③」，以及「初級英語模擬試題①②③」出版之後，受到讀者廣大的迴響，許多國中都集體訂購這兩套書，當作教科書使用，給了我們非常大的鼓勵。

　　因此我們再推出「初級英語聽力檢定④」，書中所有的對話內容，均由本公司美籍老師親筆撰寫，用字遣詞最接近美國人的說法。同學們做練習之餘，還可以將書中的句子，大聲地朗讀出來，增加語感。考聽力的時候，建議同學可以先看選項，再聽題目，遇到題目聽不懂時，要趕快放棄，先看下一題，絕對要超前錄音帶內容，先看選項，不能落後，如此才是得分關鍵。

　　本書試題全部經過劉毅英文「初級英語檢定模考班」，實際在課堂上使用過，效果奇佳。本書所有試題均附有詳細的中文翻譯及單字註解，節省讀者查字典的時間。

　　感謝這麼多讀者，給我們鼓勵。編輯好書，是「學習」一貫的宗旨，讀者若需要任何學習英文的書，都可以提供意見給我們，我們的目標是，**學英文的書**，「**學習**」都有；「**學習**」出版、天天進步。也盼望讀者們不吝給我們批評指正。

劉　毅

本書製作過程

　　本書由林銀姿老師擔任總指揮，感謝劉毅英文「初級英語檢定模考班」的同學們，在上課的八週期間，提供許多寶貴的意見，讓這些試題更加完善。感謝美籍老師 Laura E. Stewart 負責編寫考題，也要感謝謝靜芳老師再三仔細校訂，白雪嬌小姐負責封面設計，李佩姍小姐繪製插圖，黃淑貞小姐負責版面設計，蘇淑玲小姐協助打字。

全民英語能力分級檢定測驗
初級測驗①

本測驗分三部份，全爲三選一之選擇題，每部份各 10 題，共 30 題，作答時間約 20 分鐘。

第一部份：看圖辨義

本部份共 10 題，試題冊上每題有一個圖片，請聽錄音機播出一個相關的問題，與 A、B、C 三個英語敘述後，選一個與所看到圖片最相符的答案，並在答案紙上相對的圓圈內塗黑作答。每題播出一遍，問題及選項均不印在試題冊上。

例：（看）

NT$80   NT$50

（聽）

Look at the picture. How much is the hamburger?

A. It's eighty dollars.
B. It's fifty-five dollars.
C. It's eighteen dollars.

正確答案爲 A

Question 1

Question 2

Question 3

Question 4

Question 5

Question 6

請 翻 頁 ▯▯⟹

Question 7

Question 8

Question 9

Question 10

請 翻 頁 ⫸

第二部份：問答

本部份共 10 題，每題錄音機會播出一個問句或直述句，每題播出一次，聽後請從試題冊上 A、B、C 三個選項中，選出一個最適合的回答或回應，並在答案紙上塗黑作答。

例：

（聽）　Good morning, Kevin. How are you?

（看）　A.　I'm fine, thank you.
　　　　B.　I'm in the living room.
　　　　C.　My name is Kevin.

正確答案為 A

11. A. Since two o'clock.
　　B. Almost every day.
　　C. It starts at six thirty.

12. A. It's not your bag.
　　B. Thanks. You're a big help.
　　C. That will be fifty dollars, please.

13. A. Thanks.
　　B. No, I didn't.
　　C. You're welcome.

14. A. Would you like cream and sugar with that?
　　B. Here you are.
　　C. I'm not very thirsty.

15. A. My umbrella is black.
    B. It might run away.
    C. It might rain today.

16. A. I live in the next town.
    B. It's a nice town.
    C. About ten kilometers.

17. A. I go to English class twice a week.
    B. I studied English in America.
    C. I did well on the last test.

18. A. Well-done, please.
    B. Very much, thank you.
    C. With milk and a little sugar.

19. A. Yes. Your mother phoned.
    B. Call on me anytime.
    C. What are you called?

20. A. It's not red; it's blue.
    B. Yes. I read it last year.
    C. No, I haven't watched it yet.

請 翻 頁 ▌⟹

第三部份：簡短對話

本部份共 10 題，每題錄音機會播出一段對話及一個相關的問題，每題播出兩次，聽後請從試題冊上 A、B、C 三個選項中，選出一個最適合的回答，並在答案紙上塗黑作答。

例：

（聽）(Woman)　Good afternoon, …Mr. Davis?

(Man)　　　Yes.　I have an appointment with Dr. Sanders at two o'clock.　My son Tommy has a fever.

(Woman)　Oh, that's too bad.　Well, please have a seat, Mr. Davis.　Dr. Sanders will be right with you.

Question:　Where did this conversation take place?

（看）A.　In a post office.

B.　In a restaurant.

C.　In a doctor's office.

正確答案爲 C

21. A. He thinks the
　　 woman's new
　　 friend is interesting.
　 B. He thinks making
　　 friends through the
　　 Internet is not a good
　　 idea.
　 C. He thinks the woman
　　 should meet her new
　　 friend and get to
　　 know him better.

22. A. He will treat the girl
　　 to lunch.
　 B. He will help the girl
　　 with her homework.
　 C. He will finish his
　　 French homework.

23. A. 8:00 p.m.
　 B. 7:00 p.m.
　 C. 7:30 a.m.

24. A. In a restaurant.
　 B. In McDonald's.
　 C. At a noodle stand.

25. A. It is 3:10.
　 B. The boy cannot tell
　　 time.
　 C. The time shown on
　　 the clock is incorrect.

26. A. She would take a
　　 plane.
　 B. She would take a bus.
　 C. She would go the
　　 fastest way possible.

請 翻 頁 ◖⟹

27. A. In the living room.
    B. In his classroom.
    C. In his bedroom.

28. A. She will take a math test.
    B. She will play badminton.
    C. She will prepare for an exam.

29. A. They are mother and son.
    B. They are sister and brother.
    C. They are classmates.

30. A. With his friends.
    B. To the beach.
    C. He drove there.

初級英語聽力檢定①詳解

第一部份

Look at the picture for question 1.

1.(**C**) Why is the girl crying?

    A. The food is too hot.

    B. She cut her hand.

    C. She is cutting onions.

    * cut〔kʌt〕v. 割傷;切 (三態同形)

    onion〔ˋʌnjən〕n. 洋蔥

Look at the picture for question 2.

2.(**B**) What is Peter doing at Seven-Eleven?

    A. He is asking the time.

    B. He is buying some milk.

    C. He is eating ice cream.

    * *ice cream* 冰淇淋

Look at the picture for question 3.

3.(**A**) Where is the post office?

    A. It is opposite the park.

    B. There are two.

    C. You should use the crosswalk.

    * *post office* 郵局　　opposite〔ˋɑpəzɪt〕*prep.* 在…的對面

    crosswalk〔ˋkrɔs,wɔk〕n. 行人穿越道

Look at the picture for question 4.

4. (**A**) When is the girl's birthday?

    A. It is April second.

    B. Everyone forgot her birthday.

    C. She had a good time at her birthday party.

    * forget〔fɚ'gɛt〕v. 忘記
    have a good time 玩得愉快

Look at the picture for question 5.

5. (**A**) What is the cat doing in the fish tank?

    A. It is catching fish.

    B. It is washing its paw.

    C. It is on the counter.

    * tank〔tæŋk〕n. 水槽　　***fish tank*** 魚缸
    catch〔kætʃ〕v. 捉　　wash〔wɑʃ〕v. 洗
    paw〔pɔ〕n. 腳掌　　counter〔'kaʊntɚ〕n. 櫃台

Look at the picture for question 6.

6. (**B**) What is behind the house?

    A. There is one swing.

    B. There is a pond.

    C. There is a tree next to the door.

    * behind〔bɪ'haɪnd〕prep. 在…的後面
    swing〔swɪŋ〕n. 鞦韆
    pond〔pɑnd〕n. 池塘　　***next to*** 在…旁邊

Look at the picture for question 7.

7. (**A**) What time is the boy studying?

    A. He is studying at five o'clock.

    B. He has three books.

    C. He is studying at the desk.

    * *at the desk* 在書桌前

Look at the picture for question 8.

8. (**C**) Why is the boy sitting on the steps?

    A. He is very tired.

    B. He is on the second step.

    C. He forgot his key.

    * step〔stɛp〕n.（門口的）台階
      tired〔taɪrd〕adj. 疲倦的
      key〔ki〕n. 鑰匙

Look at the picture for question 9.

9. (**C**) What is the man carrying?

    A. He is wearing a hat.

    B. He has a dog.

    C. He is carrying a basket.

    * carry〔'kærɪ〕v. 攜帶
      hat〔hæt〕n.（有邊的）帽子
      basket〔'bæskɪt〕n. 籃子

Look at the picture for question 10.

10. (**C**) What is the man writing?

    A. He is a waiter.

    B. He is writing her telephone number.

    C. He is writing her order.

    * waiter〔'wetɚ〕*n.* 服務生　　order〔'ɔrdɚ〕*n.* 點餐

    well-done〔'wɛl'dʌn〕*adj.* 全熟的

第二部份

11. (**A**) How long have you been watching TV?

    A. Since two o'clock.

    B. Almost every day.

    C. It starts at six thirty.

    * since〔sɪns〕*prep.* 自從　　almost〔'ɔl‚most〕*adv.* 幾乎

12. (**B**) You can give me that bag. I'll carry it for you.

    A. It's not your bag.

    B. Thanks. You're a big help.

    C. That will be fifty dollars, please.

    * bag〔bæg〕*n.* 袋子　　help〔hɛlp〕*n.* 幫忙；幫手

13. (**A**) Here's your change, sir.

    A. Thanks.　　　　B. No, I didn't.

    C. You're welcome.

    * change〔tʃendʒ〕*n.* 零錢

    You're welcome. 不客氣。

14. (**B**) Please give me a glass of water.

     A. Would you like cream and sugar with that?

     B. Here you are.

     C. I'm not very thirsty.

     * cream〔krim〕*n.* 奶精　　sugar〔'ʃugɚ〕*n.* 糖
     Here you are. 你要的東西在這裏；拿去吧。
     (= *Here you go.* = *Here it is.*)
     thirsty〔'θɝstɪ〕*adj.* 口渴的

15. (**C**) Why are you carrying an umbrella?

     A. My umbrella is black.

     B. It might run away.

     C. It might rain today.

     * umbrella〔ʌm'brɛlə〕*n.* 雨傘
     run away 逃跑

16. (**C**) How far is it to the next town?

     A. I live in the next town.

     B. It's a nice town.

     C. About ten kilometers.

     * ***How far~?*** ～有多遠？
     next〔nɛkst〕*adj.* 下一個的
     town〔taʊn〕*n.* 城鎮
     kilometer〔'kɪlə,mitɚ〕*n.* 公里

17. (**A**) When do you study English?

    A. I go to English class twice a week.

    B. I studied English in America.

    C. I did well on the last test.

    * twice〔twaɪs〕*adv.* 兩次　　***do well*** 表現好；考得好
    last〔læst〕*adj.* 最後的；上一次的　　test〔tɛst〕*n.* 考試

18. (**C**) How would you like your coffee?

    A. Well-done, please.

    B. Very much, thank you.

    C. With milk and a little sugar.

    * ***How would you like your coffee?***
    你的咖啡要加糖還是奶精嗎？
    well-done〔'wɛl'dʌn〕*adj.* (肉)全熟的

19. (**A**) Did anyone call me?

    A. Yes. Your mother phoned.

    B. Call on me anytime.

    C. What are you called?

    * call〔kɔl〕*v.* 打電話給~ (= *phone*)；稱作
    call on 拜訪　　anytime〔'ɛnɪ,taɪm〕*adv.* 任何時候

20. (**B**) Have you read this book?

    A. It's not red; it's blue.

    B. Yes. I read it last year.

    C. No, I haven't watched it yet.

    * yet〔jɛt〕*adv.* 尚(未)

第三部份

21. (**B**) M : Where are you going?

W : I'm going to meet a new friend.

M : How do you know him?

W : I met him through the Internet. He sounds like an interesting guy.

M : But that's dangerous. You don't know anything about him.

Question : What does the man think?

A. He thinks the woman's new friend is interesting.

B. He thinks making friends through the Internet is not a good idea.

C. He thinks the woman should meet her new friend and get to know him better.

* meet〔mit〕*v.* 和～見面；認識

through〔θru〕*prep.* 透過

Internet〔'ɪntəˌnɛt〕*n.* 網路

sound〔saund〕*v.* 聽起來

interesting〔'ɪntrɪstɪŋ〕*adj.* 有趣的

guy〔gaɪ〕*n.* 人；傢伙

dangerous〔'dendʒərəs〕*adj.* 危險的

make friends 交朋友   ***get to*** + *V.* 逐漸

better〔'bɛtə〕*adv.* 更加

22. (**B**)　M：Did you finish the homework?

W：All except for the French homework.

M：I finished it last night. I can help you if you like.

W：Great. Let's work on it during lunch.

Question：What will the boy do?

A. He will treat the girl to lunch.

B. He will help the girl with her homework.

C. He will finish his French homework.

* finish〔'fɪnɪʃ〕*v.* 完成　　***except for*** 除了…之外
French〔frɛntʃ〕*n.* 法文　　***work on*** 致力於
during〔'djʊrɪŋ〕*prep.* 在…期間
treat〔trit〕*v.* 請客＜*to*＞
help *sb.* ***with*** *sth.* 幫助某人某事

23. (**B**)　W：Do you want to go swimming?

M：All right. But we'll have to hurry.

W：Why?

M：Because the pool closes at 8:00 tonight.

Question：What time did this conversation take place?

A. 8:00 p.m.

B. 7:00 p.m.

C. 7:30 a.m.

* ***go swimming*** 去游泳　　***All right*** . 好。
hurry〔'hɜɪ〕*v.* 趕快　　pool〔pul〕*n.* 游泳池
conversation〔,kɑnvɚ'seʃən〕*n.* 對話
take place 發生　　***p.m.*** 下午（↔ *a.m.* 上午）

24. (**A**)　W：How would you like your eggs?

　　　　M：Scrambled, please.

　　　　W：And do you want coffee or tea?

　　　　M：Tea, please.

　　Question：Where did this conversation take place?

　　A. In a restaurant.

　　B. In McDonald's.

　　C. At a noodle stand.

　　* **would like**　想要　　　egg〔εg〕*n.* 蛋
　　scramble〔'skræmbḷ〕*v.* 炒（蛋）
　　noodle stand 麵攤

25. (**C**)　M：That clock says it is 3:00.

　　　　W：But that clock is not right.

　　　　M：So what time is it?

　　　　W：It's ten to three.

　　Question：What is true?

　　A. It is 3:10.

　　B. The boy cannot tell time.

　　C. The time shown on the clock is incorrect.

　　* say〔se〕*v.*（鐘錶）顯示　　right〔raɪt〕*adj.* 正確的
　　It's ten to three. 現在是差十分鐘就三點；現在是兩點五十分。
　　true〔tru〕*adj.* 眞實的；正確的
　　tell〔tεl〕*v.* 看（時間）　　show〔ʃo〕*v.* 顯示
　　incorrect〔,ɪnkə'rεkt〕*adj.* 不正確的（↔ *correct*）

26. (**B**) W : How will you get to Kaohsiung?

M : I'm going to fly.

W : Isn't that expensive?

M : A little, but it's much faster.

W : I would rather save money than time.

Question : How would the woman prefer to go to Kaohsiung?

A. She would take a plane.　　B. She would take a bus.

C. She would go the fastest way possible.

* **get to** 到達　　fly〔flaɪ〕*v.* 搭飛機

a little 一點　　*would rather* 寧願

save〔sev〕*v.* 節省　　prefer〔prɪˋfɝ〕*v.* 比較喜歡

plane〔plen〕*n.* 飛機　　way〔we〕*n.* 方式

possible〔ˋpɑsəbḷ〕*adj.* 可能的

go the fastest way possible 以最快到達（目的地）的方式前往；以最節省時間的方式前往（目的地）

27. (**C**) W : Where is your brother?

M : He's in the living room.

W : No, he's not.

M : Oh. Then he must be in his room.

Question : Where does the boy think his brother is now?

A. In the living room.　　B. In his classroom.

C. In his bedroom.

* **living room** 客廳　　then〔ðɛn〕*adv.* 那麼

bedroom〔ˋbɛd͵rum〕*n.* 臥室

28. (**C**) M : Do you want to play badminton this afternoon?

W : I'd like to, but I can't. I have to study.

M : What for?

W : I have a math test tomorrow.

Question : What will the girl do this afternoon?

A. She will take a math test.

B. She will play badminton.

C. She will prepare for an exam.

* badminton (ˈbædmɪntən) *n.* 羽毛球
  What for? 爲什麼? (= *Why?*)   ***take a test*** 參加考試
  prepare (prɪˈpɛr) *v.* 準備 <*for*>
  exam (ɪgˈzæm) *n.* 考試

29. (**B**) M : Mother's Day is coming up.

W : Yes, I know. Let's go shopping tomorrow.

M : What do you think she'd like?

W : How about some perfume?

M : But we gave her that last year.

Question : What is the relationship between the boy
            and the girl?

A. They are mother and son.

B. They are sister and brother.

C. They are classmates.

* ***Mother's Day*** 母親節   ***come up*** 接近
  How about~? ~如何?   perfume (pɚˈfjum) *n.* 香水
  relationship (rɪˈleʃənˌʃɪp) *n.* 關係

30. (**B**)　W：Where did you go last weekend?

　　　　M：I went to the beach with my friends.

　　　　W：How did you get there?

　　　　M：My friend's mother drove us there.

　　　Question：Where did the boy go?

　　　A.　With his friends.

　　　B.　To the beach.

　　　C.　He drove there.

* weekend〔'wik'ɛnd〕*n.* 週末　　beach〔bitʃ〕*n.* 海灘

　drive sb. 開車載某人　　*drive there* 開車去那裡

【劉毅老師的話】

　　你想學會 KK 音標嗎？劉毅英文有特別的方法，只要一小時，就可以學會。祕訣是用已會的單字學音標，如果你會說 I (我)，你就會唸 /aɪ/ 這個音標了。其次，你要學會區別，如 æ 和 ɛ 的區別。你只要知道唸 æ 的時候，嘴巴裂開即可，訣竅一點就通。請注意我們開設的「KK 音標發音祕訣班」。

全民英語能力分級檢定測驗
初級測驗②

　　本測驗分三部份，全為三選一之選擇題，每部份各 10 題，共 30 題，作答時間約 20 分鐘。

第一部份：看圖辨義

　　本部份共 10 題，試題冊上每題有一個圖片，請聽錄音機播出一個相關的問題，與 A、B、C 三個英語敘述後，選一個與所看到圖片最相符的答案，並在答案紙上相對的圓圈內塗黑作答。每題播出一遍，問題及選項均不印在試題冊上。

例：（看）

NT$80　　NT$50

（聽）

Look at the picture.　How much is the hamburger?

　A.　It's eighty dollars.
　B.　It's fifty-five dollars.
　C.　It's eighteen dollars.

正確答案為 A

Question 1

Question 2

Question 3

Question 4

Question 5

Question 6

請 翻 頁 ⫸

Question 7

Question 8

Question 9

Question 10

請 翻 頁

第二部份： 問答

本部份共 10 題，每題錄音機會播出一個問句或直述句，
每題播出一次，聽後請從試題冊上 A、B、C 三個選項
中，選出一個最適合的回答或回應，並在答案紙上塗黑
作答。

例：

（聽） Good morning, Kevin. How are you?

（看） A. I'm fine, thank you.
　　　 B. I'm in the living room.
　　　 C. My name is Kevin.

正確答案為 A

11. A. We will take a taxi.
　　 B. It is at my friend's house.
　　 C. We will get there by seven.

12. A. Yes, I often ride one.
　　 B. No, he's not old enough.
　　 C. Yes, he is.

13. A. It feels fine.
　　 B. It's Wednesday.
　　 C. Fine, thank you.

14. A. Yes. I think she's a nice girl.
　　 B. Of course. I love Japanese food.
　　 C. Sure. Let's play a game now.

15. A. Why not try the
      bookstore?
    B. It comes from cows.
    C. At the supermarket.

16. A. And they are very
      comfortable on my
      feet, too.
    B. Thanks. They were
      a gift.
    C. No, I'm not.

17. A. I'm sorry. I don't
      have that book.
    B. It's about three
      hundred pages.
    C. I have six in my bag.

18. A. No, Diane is never
      late.
    B. Yes, I saw her five
      minutes ago.
    C. Yes, I will.

19. A. It's an express.
    B. It leaves from the
      main station.
    C. In ten minutes.

20. A. If you don't read it,
      you'll never pass
      the test.
    B. Here you are.
    C. I don't want to read
      it, either.

請 翻 頁 ⟹

第三部份：簡短對話

　　本部份共 10 題，每題錄音機會播出一段對話及一個相關的問題，每題播出兩次，聽後請從試題冊上 A、B、C 三個選項中，選出一個最適合的回答，並在答案紙上塗黑作答。

例：

（聽）(Woman)　Good afternoon, …Mr. Davis?

　　　(Man)　　Yes.　I have an appointment with Dr. Sanders at two o'clock.　My son Tommy has a fever.

　　　(Woman)　Oh, that's too bad.　Well, please have a seat, Mr. Davis.　Dr. Sanders will be right with you.

　　　Question:　Where did this conversation take place?

（看）A.　In a post office.
　　　B.　In a restaurant.
　　　C.　In a doctor's office.

正確答案爲 C

21. A. He is ten.
　　B. It is tomorrow.
　　C. She will give him a card.

22. A. It is across the street.
　　B. It is number 12.
　　C. It is far away.

23. A. The girl should read
the book.
   B. The girl should see
the movie.
   C. The girl should like
the movie.

24. A. She already played
basketball today.
   B. She has already seen
Harry Potter.
   C. *Harry Potter* is not a
good movie.

25. A. She is more than
eight years old.
   B. She goes to piano
class every day.
   C. She cannot play any
instrument.

26. A. It is cold.
   B. It is July.
   C. It is January.

27. A. Oranges are always
cheaper than apples.
   B. The woman should
buy the apples.
   C. It is not the right time
of year for apples.

28. A. He likes to watch TV.
   B. He only likes to play
sports.
   C. He likes to eat potato
chips.

29. A. On foot.
   B. Ten minutes.
   C. By bus.

30. A. The word "conscious"
can be found in the
dictionary.
   B. He likes to look words
up in the dictionary.
   C. He doesn't know how
to spell the word
"conscious," either.

請 翻 頁 ⟹

初級英語聽力檢定②詳解

第一部份

Look at the picture for question 1.

1. (**B**) What are the children eating?
   A. Story books.   B. Ice cream.
   C. Notebooks.

   * ***story book*** 故事書   ***ice cream*** 冰淇淋
   notebook ﹝'not,bʊk﹞ *n.* 筆記本

Look at the picture for question 2.

2. (**C**) Jean is on a diet. What can't she eat?
   A. She cannot eat for three weeks.
   B. She cannot eat apples.
   C. She cannot eat fast food.

   * ***on a diet*** 節食   ***fast food*** 速食

Look at the picture for question 3.

3. (**C**) What are the children doing?
   A. They are in the park.
   B. They are riding a bicycle.
   C. They are arguing.

   * argue ﹝'ɑrgjʊ﹞ *v.* 爭論

Look at the picture for question 4.

4. (**A**) What is Peter doing?

    A. He is helping a blind man.

    B. He is admiring a man's sunglasses.

    C. He is shaking a man's hand.

    * blind〔blaɪnd〕*adj.* 眼盲的

      admire〔əd'maɪr〕*v.* 讚賞

      sunglasses〔'sʌn͵glæsɪz〕*n. pl.* 太陽眼鏡

      shake〔ʃek〕*v.* 握（手）

Look at the picture for question 5.

5. (**B**) Where is the man sleeping?

    A. In the newspaper.

    B. On the bench.

    C. In the trees.

    * bench〔bɛntʃ〕*n.* 長椅

Look at the picture for question 6.

6. (**B**) What is the boy fixing?

    A. It is broken.

    B. It is a computer.

    C. It is very difficult.

    * fix〔fɪks〕*v.* 修理

      broken〔'brokən〕*adj.* 故障的

      computer〔kəm'pjutɚ〕*n.* 電腦

      difficult〔'dɪfə͵kʌlt〕*adj.* 困難的

Look at the picture for question 7.

7. (**C**)　Why is Jack sad?

　　　A. He cannot sell the tickets.

　　　B. The tickets are too expensive.

　　　C. There are no more tickets.

　　* sad〔sæd〕*adj.* 難過的

　　　ticket〔'tɪkɪt〕*n.* 彩券

　　　sell out 賣完

Look at the picture for question 8.

8. (**B**)　What is the woman?

　　　A. She is a flight attendant.

　　　B. She is a travel agent.

　　　C. She is a passenger.

　　* ***What is*** *sb.***?** 某人的職業是什麼？

　　　attendant〔ə'tɛndənt〕*n.* 服務員

　　　flight attendant 空服員　　agent〔'edʒənt〕*n.* 代辦人

　　　travel agent 旅行代辦人

　　　passenger〔'pæsṇdʒɚ〕*n.* 乘客

Look at the picture for question 9.

9. (**A**)　What class is this?

　　　A. Math.

　　　B. Drawing.

　　　C. Confused.

　　* math〔mæθ〕*n.* 數學　　drawing〔'drɔ·ɪŋ〕*n.* 畫圖

　　　confused〔kən'fjuzd〕*adj.* 困惑的

Look at the picture for question 10.

10. (**B**) Who is the woman?

      A. A movie star.   B. A bride.

      C. A marriage.

      * star〔star〕*n.* 明星

        bride〔braɪd〕*n.* 新娘   marriage〔'mærɪdʒ〕*n.* 婚禮

第二部份

11. (**A**) How will you get to the party?

      A. We will take a taxi.

      B. It is at my friend's house.

      C. We will get there by seven.

      * ***get to*** 到達   take〔tek〕*v.* 搭乘

        by〔baɪ〕*prep.* 在…之前

12. (**B**) Does your brother drive a motorcycle?

      A. Yes, I often ride one.

      B. No, he's not old enough.

      C. Yes, he is.

      * drive〔draɪv〕*v.* 駕駛

        motorcycle〔'motə‚saɪkl̩〕*n.* 摩托車   ride〔raɪd〕*v.* 騎

13. (**C**) How do you feel today?

      A. It feels fine.   B. It's Wednesday.

      C. Fine, thank you.

      * feel〔fil〕*v.* 感覺；摸起來

14. (**B**) Do you like sushi?

    A. Yes. I think she's a nice girl.

    B. Of course. I love Japanese food.

    C. Sure. Let's play a game now.

    * sushi〔'suʃɪ〕*n.* 壽司　　Japanese〔ˌdʒæpə'niz〕*adj.* 日本的

15. (**C**) Where can I buy some milk?

    A. Why not try the bookstore?

    B. It comes from cows.

    C. At the supermarket.

    * *Why not~?* 爲何不~？（表建議）

    bookstore〔'buk,stor〕*n.* 書店　　cow〔kau〕*n.* 母牛

    supermarket〔'supə,markɪt〕*n.* 超級市場

16. (**B**) What a beautiful pair of earrings!

    A. And they are very comfortable on my feet, too.

    B. Thanks. They were a gift.

    C. No, I'm not.

    * pair〔pɛr〕*n.* 一對　　earrings〔'ɪr,rɪŋz〕*n. pl.* 耳環

    comfortable〔'kʌmfətəbl̩〕*adj.* 舒服的

    gift〔gɪft〕*n.* 禮物

17. (**C**) How many books do you have?

    A. I'm sorry. I don't have that book.

    B. It's about three hundred pages.

    C. I have six in my bag.

    * page〔pedʒ〕*n.* 頁

18. (**B**) Have you seen Diane lately?

    A. No, Diane is never late.

    B. Yes, I saw her five minutes ago.

    C. Yes, I will.

    * lately (ˈletlɪ) adv. 最近

      late (let) adj. 遲到的

      minute (ˈmɪnɪt) n. 分鐘

19. (**C**) When will the train leave?

    A. It's an express.

    B. It leaves from the main station.

    C. In ten minutes.

    * leave (liv) v. 離開；出發

      express (ɪkˈsprɛs) n. 快車

      main (men) adj. 主要的　　*main station* 總站

      In ten minutes. 再過十分鐘。

20. (**B**) Please pass me that book.

    A. If you don't read it, you'll never pass the test.

    B. Here you are.

    C. I don't want to read it, either.

    * pass (pæs) v. 傳遞；通過（考試）

      Here you are. 你要的東西在這裡；拿去吧。

      (= *Here it is.* = *Here you go.*)

      either (ˈiðɚ) adv. 也（不）

第三部份

21. (**B**) M：That's a nice card. Is it someone's birthday?

W：Yes. It's my little brother's.

M：How old is he?

W：He'll be ten tomorrow.

Question：When is the girl's brother's birthday?

A. He is ten.

B. It is tomorrow.

C. She will give him a card.

* card〔kɑrd〕*n.* 卡片

22. (**C**) M：Excuse me, do you know where the museum is?

W：Yes, but it's really too far to walk. You'd better take a bus.

M：Which bus should I take?

W：You can take number 12 from across the street.

Question：Where is the museum?

A. It is across the street.

B. It is number 12.

C. It is far away.

* museum〔mju'ziəm〕*n.* 博物館

too…to V. 太…以致於不～

had better + 原形 *V*. 最好

across〔ə'krɔs〕*prep.* 在…對面

far away 遙遠的

23. (**B**) W : Have you read the book, *The Lord of the Rings*?

　　　　 M : No, but I've seen the movie.

　　　　 W : Did you like it?

　　　　 M : Yes. You should go see it.

　　　　 Question : What does the boy mean?

　　　　 A. The girl should read the book.

　　　　 B. The girl should see the movie.

　　　　 C. The girl should like the movie.

　　　　 * lord〔lɔrd〕*n.* 主人　　ring〔rɪŋ〕*n.* 戒指
　　　　 　The Lord of the Rings 魔戒（電影及小說名）

24. (**B**) M : Are you going to play basketball tonight?

　　　　 W : No, I'm going to the movies.

　　　　 M : Are you going to see *Harry Potter*?

　　　　 W : No, I saw that one last week.

　　　　 Question : What does the girl mean?

　　　　 A. She already played basketball today.

　　　　 B. She has already seen *Harry Potter*.

　　　　 C. *Harry Potter* is not a good movie.

　　　　 * *go to the movies* 去看電影

25. (**A**) M：Where are you going?

W：I'm going to my piano class.

M：How long have you been playing the piano?

W：Since I was eight years old.

Question：What do we know about the girl?

A. She is more than eight years old.

B. She goes to piano class every day.

C. She cannot play any instrument.

* since〔sɪns〕*conj.* 自從　　*more than* 超過

instrument〔'ɪnstrəmənt〕*n.* 樂器（= *musical instrument*）

26. (**C**) W：How often do you go swimming?

M：I go every day in summer, but now I only swim

twice a week.

W：I don't like to swim at all when it's this cold.

Question：What month is it?

A. It is cold.

B. It is July.

C. It is January.

* *How often～?* ～多久一次？（問頻率）

go swimming 去游泳

twice〔twaɪs〕*adv.* 兩次　　*not…at all* 一點也不

this〔ðɪs〕*adv.* 到這樣的程度　　*this cold* 這麼冷

month〔mʌnθ〕*n.* 月份

27. (**C**) W：Which are cheaper, the apples or the oranges?

M：The oranges are much cheaper at this time of year.

W：Why is that?

M：Apples are not in season now.

Question：What does the man mean?

A. Oranges are always cheaper than apples.

B. The woman should buy the apples.

C. It is not the right time of year for apples.

* *in season* （水果）當季的；盛產期的（↔ *out of season* ）

right〔raɪt〕*adj.* 合適的；恰當的

28. (**A**) W：What kind of exercise do you like to do?

M：I don't like to exercise. I'm really just a

couch potato.

W：Don't you like sports?

M：Sure, I do. But I like to watch them, not play them.

Question：What does the boy like?

A. He likes to watch TV.

B. He only likes to play sports.

C. He likes to eat potato chips.

* kind〔kaɪnd〕*n.* 種類　　exercise〔'ɛksɚ͵saɪz〕*n. v.* 運動

couch〔kautʃ〕*n.* 長沙發　　potato〔pə'teto〕*n.* 馬鈴薯

couch potato 成天坐在沙發上看電視的懶人

potato chips 洋芋片

29. (**B**) M : How far is it to your house from here?

W : It's about a ten-minute walk.

M : You're so lucky! I have to take a bus to school.

Question : How long does it take the girl to get to school?

A. On foot.

B. Ten minutes.

C. By bus.

* *How far~?* ~多遠？（問距離）
  walk〔wɔk〕*n.* 步行的路程
  a ten-minute walk 步行十分鐘
  lucky〔ˈlʌkɪ〕*adj.* 幸運的
  How long~? ~多久？（問時間） *on foot* 步行

30. (**C**) W : Can you hand me that dictionary?

M : Sure. What are you looking for?

W : I need to know how to spell the word "conscious."

M : Oh. I'd have to look that up, too.

Question : What does the boy mean?

A. The word "conscious" can be found in the dictionary.

B. He likes to look words up in the dictionary.

C. He doesn't know how to spell the word "conscious," either.

* hand〔hænd〕*v.* 拿給
  dictionary〔ˈdɪkʃən͵ɛrɪ〕*n.* 字典
  look for 尋找　　spell〔spɛl〕*v.* 拼（字）
  conscious〔ˈkɑnʃəs〕*adj.* 有意識的　　*look up* 查閱

全民英語能力分級檢定測驗
初級測驗③

　　本測驗分三部份，全為三選一之選擇題，每部份各 10 題，共 30 題，作答時間約 20 分鐘。

第一部份：看圖辨義

　　　　　本部份共 10 題，試題冊上每題有一個圖片，請聽錄音機播出一個相關的問題，與 A、B、C 三個英語敘述後，選一個與所看到圖片最相符的答案，並在答案紙上相對的圓圈內塗黑作答。每題播出一遍，問題及選項均不印在試題冊上。

例：（看）

NT$80　　NT$50

（聽）

Look at the picture.　How much is the hamburger?

　　A.　It's eighty dollars.
　　B.　It's fifty-five dollars.
　　C.　It's eighteen dollars.

正確答案為 A

Question 1

Question 2

Question 3

Question 4

Question 5

Question 6

請翻頁 ▉⟹

Question 7

Question 8

Question 9

Question 10

請 翻 頁 ⫸

第二部份：問答

本部份共10題，每題錄音機會播出一個問句或直述句，每題播出一次，聽後請從試題冊上 A、B、C 三個選項中，選出一個最適合的回答或回應，並在答案紙上塗黑作答。

例：

（聽） Good morning, Kevin. How are you?

（看） A. I'm fine, thank you.
B. I'm in the living room.
C. My name is Kevin.

正確答案為 A

11. A. That's wonderful.
B. Was he hurt?
C. I didn't mean it.

12. A. Where is it?
B. Have some ice cream.
C. You should exercise more.

13. A. 20 pages.
B. 100 years.
C. It's due tomorrow.

14. A. I passes the final exam.
B. I want to find a job.
C. It will finish at 12:00.

15. A. I can swim very well.
    B. It was too cold.
    C. It's my favorite sport.

16. A. Please do.
    B. Where do you want
       to go?
    C. No thanks, I'm full.

17. A. He is doing his
       homework.
    B. He likes fishing.
    C. He is still a student.

18. A. That's all right.
    B. You did very well.
    C. I'm so proud of you.

19. A. You should take a rest.
    B. You should stop to
       talk.
    C. You should throw it
       away.

20. A. On the radio.
    B. About an hour ago.
    C. Yes, it was terrible.

請 翻 頁 〗⟹

第三部份：　簡短對話

本部份共 10 題，每題錄音機會播出一段對話及一個相關的問題，每題播出兩次，聽後請從試題冊上 A、B、C 三個選項中，選出一個最適合的回答，並在答案紙上塗黑作答。

例：

（聽）（Woman）Good afternoon, …Mr. Davis?

（Man）　　Yes.　I have an appointment with Dr. Sanders at two o'clock.　My son Tommy has a fever.

（Woman）Oh, that's too bad.　Well, please have a seat, Mr. Davis.　Dr. Sanders will be right with you.

Question:　Where did this conversation take place?

（看）A.　In a post office.

　　　B.　In a restaurant.

　　　C.　In a doctor's office.

正確答案為 C

21. A. Yes, he does.
　　B. It's math.
　　C. Yes, he is.

22. A. Ride a bike.
　　B. Roller-skate.
　　C. Teach the girl.

23. A. He never eats French fries.
    B. It is cheaper than the French fries.
    C. He is trying to lose weight.

24. A. Help the girl to meet the new boy.
    B. Invite the girl to the new boy's classroom.
    C. Ask the girl to find the new boy.

25. A. Barbecued chicken.
    B. Steak.
    C. Fruit salad.

26. A. It is a present for the boy.
    B. It is for the girl's older brother.
    C. It is for the girl's little sister.

27. A. The price is too high.
    B. The quality is very good.
    C. He wants a free one.

28. A. Her father will not eat dinner.
    B. She will eat dinner at six thirty.
    C. She will eat dinner after seven o'clock.

29. A. Somebody broke the girl's bike.
    B. The girl no longer has a bike.
    C. The boy stole the girl's bike.

30. A. A parking ticket.
    B. A speeding ticket.
    C. A concert ticket.

請 翻 頁 ⟹

初級英語聽力檢定③詳解

第一部份

Look at the picture for question 1.

1. (**B**) How many boys are playing?
   A. These are five boys.
   B. These are four players.
   C. They are playing basketball.

   * player (′pleɚ) *n.* 球員

Look at the picture for question 2.

2. (**C**) What is the police officer doing?
   A. He is teaching the boy how to drive.
   B. He is giving the boy some money.
   C. He is writing a ticket.

   * *police officer* 警察　　drive (draɪv) *v.* 開車
   ticket (′tɪkɪt) *n.* 罰單　　*write a ticket* 開罰單

Look at the picture for question 3.

3. (**A**) What does the boy want to do?
   A. He wants to milk the cow.
   B. He wants to play with the baby cows.
   C. He wants to wash the cows.

   * milk (mɪlk) *v.* 擠（牛、羊等的）奶
   cow (kaʊ) *n.* 母牛　　*baby cow* 幼牛
   wash (waʃ) *v.* 洗

Look at the picture for question 4.

4. (**B**) What is the man?

    A. He is a pilot.

    B. He is a passenger.

    C. He is a travel agent.

    * pilot〔'paɪlət〕 *n.* 飛行員
      passenger〔'pæsṇdʒɚ〕 *n.* 乘客
      travel〔'trævḷ〕 *n.* 旅行   agent〔'edʒənt〕 *n.* 代理人
      travel agent 旅遊代辦人   passport〔'pæsˌport〕 *n.* 護照

Look at the picture for question 5.

5. (**C**) What does the police officer have?

    A. He has a motorcycle.

    B. He is waving.

    C. He has a whistle.

    * motorcycle〔'motɚˌsaɪkḷ〕 *n.* 摩托車
      wave〔wev〕 *v.* 揮手   whistle〔'hwɪsḷ〕 *n.* 哨子

Look at the picture for question 6.

6. (**B**) How much does the drink cost?

    A. It is a fast-food restaurant.

    B. It is 20 dollars.

    C. It is on the counter.

    * drink〔drɪŋk〕 *n.* 飲料
      cost〔kɔst〕 *v.* 需要（…錢）；值（…錢）
      fast-food restaurant 速食店
      counter〔'kaʊntɚ〕 *n.* 櫃台

Look at the picture for question 7.

7. (**C**) What number bus is this?
   A. There are five passengers.
   B. It is very fast.
   C. It is number 220.

Look at the picture for question 8.

8. (**B**) What does the boy want?
   A. He wants to buy the car.
   B. He wants to borrow the car.
   C. He wants to give his father the car.

   * borrow〔'baro〕*v.* 借（入）
     lend〔lɛnd〕*v.* 借（出）

Look at the picture for question 9.

9. (**A**) What did the man forget?
   A. His umbrella.
   B. His bag.
   C. His radio.

   * forget〔fɚ'gɛt〕*v.* 忘記
     umbrella〔ʌm'brɛlə〕*n.* 雨傘
     bag〔bæg〕*n.* 袋子
     radio〔'redɪo〕*n.* 收音機；廣播
     radio station 廣播電台

Look at the picture for question 10.

10. (**B**) What will the boy do?

    A. He will cook dinner.

    B. He will dry his shirt.

    C. He will clean the machine.

    * cook〔kʊk〕v. 煮　　dry〔draɪ〕v. 弄乾
      shirt〔ʃɜt〕n. 襯衫　　　clean〔klin〕v. 清理
      machine〔məˈʃin〕n. 機器

第二部份

11. (**B**) Peter was in an accident last night.

    A. That's wonderful.

    B. Was he hurt?

    C. I didn't mean it.

    * accident〔ˈæksədənt〕n. 意外
      wonderful〔ˈwʌndɚfəl〕adj. 很棒的
      hurt〔hɜt〕v. 使受傷（三態同形）
      be hurt 受傷（= *get hurt*）　　mean〔min〕v. 意圖
      I didn't mean it. 我不是那個意思；我不是故意的。

12. (**C**) I want to lose weight.

    A. Where is it?

    B. Have some ice cream.

    C. You should exercise more.

    * weight〔wet〕n. 體重　　*lose weight* 減肥
      have〔hæv〕v. 吃　　*ice cream* 冰淇淋
      exercise〔ˈɛksɚˌsaɪz〕v. 運動

13. (**A**) How long is the history chapter?

    A. 20 pages.

    B. 100 years.

    C. It's due tomorrow.

    * history〔'hɪstrɪ〕*n.* 歷史

      chapter〔'tʃæptə〕*n.*（書籍的）章

      page〔pedʒ〕*n.* 頁

      due〔dju〕*adj.* 到期的

14. (**B**) What will you do after graduation?

    A. I passed the final exam.

    B. I want to find a job.

    C. It will finish at 12:00.

    * graduation〔,grædʒʊ'eʃən〕*n.* 畢業

      pass〔pæs〕*v.* 通過（考試）

      final exam 期末考

      job〔dʒɑb〕*n.* 工作

      finish〔'fɪnɪʃ〕*v.* 結束

15. (**B**) Why didn't you go swimming?

    A. I can swim very well.

    B. It was too cold.

    C. It's my favorite sport.

    * swim〔swɪm〕*v.* 游泳

      favorite〔'fevərɪt〕*adj.* 最喜愛的

      sport〔sport〕*n.* 運動

16. (**A**) May I come in?

    A. Please do.

    B. Where do you want to go?

    C. No thanks, I'm full.

    * ***Please do***. 請進（在此等於 Please come in.）
      full〔fʊl〕*adj.* 吃飽的

17. (**C**) What does your brother do?

    A. He is doing his homework.

    B. He likes fishing.

    C. He is still a student.

    * ***What does*** *sb*. ***do?*** 某人從事什麼工作？
      homework〔'hom,wɝk〕*n.* 家庭作業　　fish〔fɪʃ〕*v.* 釣魚

18. (**A**) I'm sorry. It was an accident.

    A. That's all right.

    B. You did very well.

    C. I'm so proud of you.

    * ***That's all right***. 沒關係。
      do well 表現好　　***be proud of*** 以⋯為榮

19. (**A**) I have a sore throat.

    A. You should take a rest.

    B. You should stop to talk.

    C. You should throw it away.

    * sore〔sor〕*adj.* 疼痛的　　throat〔θrot〕*n.* 喉嚨
      have a sore throat 喉嚨痛　　***take a rest*** 休息一下
      stop to *V*. 停下來，去～　　***throw away*** 扔掉

20. (**B**) When did you hear the news?

    A. On the radio.   B. About an hour ago.

    C. Yes, it was terrible.

    * terrible〔ˈtɛrəb!〕 *adj.* 可怕的

第三部份

21. (**C**) W：Where is John?

    M：He's in the living room.

    W：What's he doing?

    M：He's doing his math homework.

    Question：Is John doing homework now?

    A. Yes, he does.   B. It's math.

    C. Yes, he is.

    * *living room* 客廳   math〔mæθ〕 *n.* 數學

22. (**B**) M：Can you ride a bike?

    W：No, I can't. But I can roller-skate.

    M：I can't do that. Can you teach me?

    Question：What is the boy unable to do?

    A. Ride a bike.   B. Roller-skate.

    C. Teach the girl.

    * bike〔baɪk〕 *n.* 腳踏車（= *bicycle*）

    roller-skate〔ˈrolɚˌsket〕 *v.* 溜冰

    unable〔ʌnˈeb!〕 *adj.* 不能…的（↔ *able*）

    be unable to V. 不能～；不會～（↔ *be able to V.*）

23. (**C**)　M：What comes with the meal?

　　　W：Salad or fries.　Which would you like?

　　　M：A salad, please.　I'm on a diet.

Question：Why does the man order the salad?

A.　He never eats French fries.

B.　It is cheaper than the French fries.

C.　He is trying to lose weight.

* meal〔mil〕*n.* 一餐
  What comes with the meal? 副餐是什麼？
  salad〔'sæləd〕*n.* 沙拉
  fries〔fraɪz〕*n. pl.* 薯條（= *French fries*）
  be on a diet 節食；減肥（= *go on a diet*）
  order〔'ɔrdɚ〕*v.* 點（餐）

24. (**A**)　M：Look.　There's the new boy in our class.

　　　　　He's very interesting, isn't he?

　　　W：I don't know.　I haven't met him yet.

　　　M：Come on.　I'll introduce you.

Question：What will the boy do？

A.　Help the girl to meet the new boy.

B.　Invite the girl to the new boy's classroom.

C.　Ask the girl to find the new boy.

* ***Look.*** 你看。（用於引起對方注意）
  interesting〔'ɪntrɪstɪŋ〕*adj.* 有趣的
  meet〔mit〕*v.* 認識　　yet〔jɛt〕*adv.* 還（沒）
  Come on. 來吧。　　introduce〔,ɪntrə'djus〕*v.* 介紹
  invite〔ɪn'vaɪt〕*v.* 邀請　　ask〔æsk〕*v.* 要求

25. (**C**) W：What are you going to do on Saturday?

M：I'm going on a picnic with my family.

W：Are you going to have a barbecue?

M：No. Fires aren't allowed in the park.

Question：What can the boy eat at the picnic?

A. Barbecued chicken.

B. Steak.

C. Fruit salad.

> * ***go on a picnic*** 去野餐
> barbecue〔'bɑrbɪ,kju〕*n. v.* 烤肉
> fire〔faɪr〕*n.*（為烹調而生的）火
> allow〔ə'laʊ〕*v.* 允許　　chicken〔'tʃɪkən〕*n.* 雞肉
> steak〔stek〕*n.* 牛排

26. (**C**) M：What did you buy?

W：I bought a teddy bear at the toy store.

M：Aren't you a little old for teddy bears?

W：It's not for me. My sister's birthday is next week.

Question：Who is the teddy bear for?

A. It is a present for the boy.

B. It is for the girl's older brother.

C. It is for the girl's little sister.

> * ***teddy bear*** 泰迪熊　　***toy store*** 玩具店
> ***a little*** 一點　　present〔'prɛzn̩t〕*n.* 禮物
> ***older brother*** 哥哥（＝*elder brother*）
> ***little sister*** 妹妹（＝*younger sister*）

27. (**A**)　M：How much is this shirt?

W：It's 500 dollars.

M：Oh.　That's a little expensive for me.　Can you give me a discount?

Question：What does the man think about the shirt?

A.　The price is too high.

B.　The quality is very good.

C.　He wants a free one.

* shirt〔ʃɜt〕*n.* 襯衫

expensive〔ɪk'spɛnsɪv〕*adj.* 昂貴的

discount〔'dɪskaʊnt〕*n.* 折扣

think about 認爲　　price〔praɪs〕*n.* 價格

quality〔'kwɑlətɪ〕*n.* 品質　　free〔fri〕*adj.* 免費的

28. (**C**)　W：What time do you usually eat dinner?

M：We usually eat at six thirty.　How about you?

W：We usually eat at seven, but tonight my father will be late.

Question：What does the girl imply?

A.　Her father will not eat dinner.

B.　She will eat dinner at six thirty.

C.　She will eat dinner after seven o'clock.

* usually〔'juʒʊəlɪ〕*adv.* 通常

How about you? 那你呢？

late〔let〕*adj.* 遲的　　imply〔ɪm'plaɪ〕*v.* 暗示

29. (**B**) M : Why were you late for school today?

W : I usually ride my bike to school but today I had to walk.

M : Is your bike broken?

W : No. Somebody stole it.

Question : What do we know?

A. Somebody broke the girl's bike.

B. The girl no longer has a bike.

C. The boy stole the girl's bike.

* broken〔'brokən〕*adj.* 故障的

steal〔stil〕*v.* 偷（三態變化為：steal-stole-stolen）

break〔brek〕*v.* 弄壞　***no longer*** 不再

30. (**B**) W : You look upset. What happened?

M : I got a traffic ticket today.

W : What for?

M : I was driving too fast.

Question : What kind of ticket did the man get?

A. A parking ticket.

B. A speeding ticket.

C. A concert ticket.

* upset〔ʌp'sɛt〕*adj.* 心煩的　happen〔'hæpən〕*v.* 發生

ticket〔'tɪkɪt〕*n.* 罰單；入場券　***traffic ticket*** 交通罰單

What for? 為什麼？（= *Why?*）　kind〔kaɪnd〕*n.* 種類

park〔pɑrk〕*v.* 停車　***parking ticket*** 違規停車罰單

speed〔spid〕*v.* 加速；超速駕駛

speeding ticket 超速罰單　concert〔'kɑnsɝt〕*n.* 演唱會

全民英語能力分級檢定測驗

初級測驗④

本測驗分三部份，全為三選一之選擇題，每部份各 10 題，共 30 題，作答時間約 20 分鐘。

第一部份：看圖辨義

本部份共 10 題，試題冊上每題有一個圖片，請聽錄音機播出一個相關的問題，與 A、B、C 三個英語敘述後，選一個與所看到圖片最相符的答案，並在答案紙上相對的圓圈內塗黑作答。每題播出一遍，問題及選項均不印在試題冊上。

例：（看）

NT$80　　NT$50

（聽）

Look at the picture. How much is the hamburger?

A. It's eighty dollars.
B. It's fifty-five dollars.
C. It's eighteen dollars.

正確答案為 A

Question 1

Question 2

Question 3

Question 4

Question 5

Question 6

請翻頁 ▯▯▯⇒

Question 7

Question 8

Question 9

Question 10

請 翻 頁 ⬛⟹

第二部份： 問答

本部份共 10 題，每題錄音機會播出一個問句或直述句，
每題播出一次，聽後請從試題冊上 A、B、C 三個選項
中，選出一個最適合的回答或回應，並在答案紙上塗黑
作答。

例：

（聽） Good morning, Kevin. How are you?

（看）　A.　I'm fine, thank you.
　　　　B.　I'm in the living room.
　　　　C.　My name is Kevin.

正確答案為 A

11. A. About an hour ago.
    B. I did it at three
       o'clock.
    C. Because I missed
       the bus.

12. A. I don't need to go
       there.
    B. I have to babysit my
       younger brother.
    C. I can go by myself.

13. A. I don't live here.
    B. No, it's too far away.
    C. Yes, I'd like to see
       your house.

14. A. I found him in a
       pet store.
    B. He was very
       expensive.
    C. I will buy him a
       new toy.

15. A. I didn't forget. The
date is May 12.
B. Sorry. I missed the
train.
C. Forget about it.

16. A. You should be more
careful.
B. Don't be angry. I
didn't do it on
purpose.
C. That's terrible. Is he
all right?

17. A. In junior high school.
B. At the park.
C. Every day.

18. A. Yes, they are all still
living.
B. In Taichung.
C. Until age seventy-
eight.

19. A. Phones are expensive
if they're not on sale.
B. No, they're too
expensive.
C. What's the number?

20. A. You're welcome any
time.
B. My grandmother
usually does.
C. Thanks. I'd love to.

請 翻 頁 ⬅⇒

第三部份： 簡短對話

本部份共 10 題，每題錄音機會播出一段對話及一個相關的問題，每題播出兩次，聽後請從試題冊上 A、B、C 三個選項中，選出一個最適合的回答，並在答案紙上塗黑作答。

例：

（聽）(Woman) Good afternoon, …Mr. Davis?

(Man) Yes. I have an appointment with Dr. Sanders at two o'clock. My son Tommy has a fever.

(Woman) Oh, that's too bad. Well, please have a seat, Mr. Davis. Dr. Sanders will be right with you.

Question: Where did this conversation take place?

（看）A. In a post office.

B. In a restaurant.

C. In a doctor's office.

正確答案爲 C

21. A. He got too tired.
    B. He caught a cold.
    C. He hit his head.

22. A. She can swim.
    B. She can play volleyball.
    C. She can snorkel.

23. A. In a beauty salon.
    B. In a dress shop.
    C. In a kitchen.

24. A. Take a walk.
    B. Eat a snack.
    C. Have a cigarette.

25. A. It is sold with the pants.
    B. It matches the pants.
    C. It doesn't go with the first shirt.

26. A. In a street market.
    B. In a shopping mall.
    C. In a bookstore.

27. A. At least ten minutes.
    B. One minute.
    C. Less than five minutes.

28. A. He stayed up studying last night and was too tired.
    B. He doesn't like to jog in the morning.
    C. He was sleeping this morning.

29. A. He lost his glasses.
    B. His eyesight is much better now.
    C. He wears contacts instead of glasses.

30. A. Help the girl find the library.
    B. Give the girl some math tips.
    C. Listen to the girl's excuses.

初級英語聽力檢定④詳解

第一部份

Look at the picture for question 1.

1. (**C**) What is on the cars?
    A. There are four.
    B. They are driving.
    C. They are flags.

   * drive〔draɪv〕v. 開車 flag〔flæg〕n. 旗子

Look at the picture for question 2.

2. (**A**) What is the boy doing?
    A. He is collecting rocks.
    B. He is picking fruit.
    C. He is eating lunch.

   * collect〔kə'lɛkt〕v. 收集 rock〔rɑk〕n. 石頭
     pick〔pɪk〕v. 摘 fruit〔frut〕n. 水果

Look at the picture for question 3.

3. (**B**) What does the woman want to do?
    A. Take a shower.
    B. Wash the carrots.
    C. Grow the carrots.

   * *take a shower* 淋浴 wash〔wɑʃ〕v. 洗
     carrot〔'kærət〕n. 紅蘿蔔 grow〔gro〕v. 種植

Look at the picture for question 4.

4. (**B**) What is wrong with the boy's pants?
   A. They are too expensive.
   B. There is a hole in them.
   C. They are dirty.

   * ***What is wrong with~?*** ～怎麼了？
     (*= What is the matter with~?*)
     pants (pænts) *n. pl.* 褲子
     expensive (ɪk'spɛnsɪv) *adj.* 昂貴的
     hole (hol) *n.* 洞　　dirty ('dɜtɪ) *adj.* 髒的

Look at the picture for question 5.

5. (**A**) How many children can jump rope?
   A. Two.
   B. There are four jump ropes.
   C. They are very tired.

   * jump (dʒʌmp) *v.* 跳　　rope (rop) *n.* 繩子
     jump rope 跳繩　　tired (taɪrd) *adj.* 疲倦的

Look at the picture for question 6.

6. (**C**) What did the father buy?
   A. He bought a rabbit.
   B. They are for his daughter.
   C. They are balloons.

   * rabbit ('ræbɪt) *n.* 兔子　　daughter ('dɔtɚ) *n.* 女兒
     balloon (bə'lun) *n.* 汽球

Look at the picture for question 7.

7. (**B**) Why did the driver stop?

    A. There is one driver.

    B. The children were playing in the street.

    C. He wants the ball.

    * driver〔'draɪvɚ〕 n. 駕駛人   stop〔stɑp〕 v. 停下來

Look at the picture for question 8.

8. (**B**) What is the woman?

    A. She is in a kitchen.

    B. She is a cook.

    C. She is hungry.

    * ***What is sb.?*** 某人從事什麼工作？

    cook〔kuk〕 n. 廚師

    hungry〔'hʌŋgrɪ〕 adj. 飢餓的

Look at the picture for question 9.

9. (**A**) How does the girl feel?

    A. She is afraid.

    B. She is cold.

    C. She is angry.

    * feel〔fil〕 v. 覺得   afraid〔ə'fred〕 adj. 害怕的

    angry〔'æŋgrɪ〕 adj. 生氣的

Look at the picture for question 10.

10. (**C**) What is the man selling?

A. He is a vendor.

B. She wants one.

C. It is fruit.

* vendor 〔'vɛndɚ〕 n. 小販

第二部份

11. (**A**) When did you get here?

A. About an hour ago.

B. I did it at three o'clock.

C. Because I missed the bus.

* *get here* 到這裡　　miss 〔mɪs〕 v. 錯過

12. (**B**) Why can't you go to the party?

A. I don't need to go there.

B. I have to babysit my younger brother.

C. I can go by myself.

* babysit 〔'bebɪ,sɪt〕 v. 當…的臨時褓姆
younger brother 弟弟　　*by oneself* 獨自；靠自己

13. (**B**) Can you see your house from here?

A. I don't live here.

B. No, it's too far away.

C. Yes, I'd like to see your house.

* *far away* 遙遠的　　*would like to V.* 想要～

14. (**A**) Where did you buy your dog?

    A. I found him in a pet store.

    B. He was very expensive.

    C. I will buy him a new toy.

    * pet〔pɛt〕n. 寵物　　toy〔tɔɪ〕n. 玩具

15. (**B**) Where were you yesterday? Did you forget our date?

    A. I didn't forget. The date is May 12.

    B. Sorry. I missed the train.

    C. Forget about it.

    * forget〔fɚ'gɛt〕v. 忘記　　date〔det〕n. 約會；日期
    Forget about it. 算不了什麼；不用謝了。

16. (**C**) My brother was in a traffic accident yesterday.

    A. You should be more careful.

    B. Don't be angry. I didn't do it on purpose.

    C. That's terrible. Is he all right?

    * traffic〔'træfɪk〕n. 交通　　accident〔'æksədənt〕n. 意外
    careful〔'kɛrfəl〕adj. 小心的
    purpose〔'pɝpəs〕n. 目的　　***on purpose*** 故意地
    terrible〔'tɛrəbḷ〕adj. 可怕的　　***all right*** 安然無恙的

17. (**A**) When did you first meet Ken?

    A. In junior high school.

    B. At the park.

    C. Every day.

    * meet〔mit〕v. 遇見

18. (**B**) Where do your grandparents live?

    A. Yes, they are all still living.

    B. In Taichung.

    C. Until age seventy-eight.

    * grandparents（'grænd,pɛrənts）*n. pl.*（外）祖父母
    living（'lɪvɪŋ）*adj.* 活著的   ***Taichung*** 台中
    until（ən'tɪl）*prep.* 直到   age（edʒ）*n.* 年齡
    age + 數字 ～歲

19. (**B**) Do you have a cell phone?

    A. Phones are expensive if they're not on sale.

    B. No, they're too expensive.

    C. What's the number?

    * ***cell phone*** 手機   ***on sale*** 特價
    number（'nʌmbɚ）*n.* 電話號碼

20. (**B**) Who cooks dinner at your house?

    A. You're welcome any time.

    B. My grandmother usually does.

    C. Thanks. I'd love to.

    * welcome（'wɛlkəm）*adj.* 受歡迎的
    grandmother（'græn,mʌðɚ）*n.*（外）祖母
    usually（'juʒʊəlɪ）*adv.* 通常
    I'd love to. 我很樂意。(= *I'd like to.*)

第三部份

21. (**B**) W：How do you feel?

　　　　M：Much better, thanks. My headache is gone and
　　　　　　I've stopped coughing.

　　　　W：But you still look tired. You should rest today.

　　　　Question：What happened to the boy?

　　　　A. He got too tired.　　B. He caught a cold.
　　　　C. He hit his head.

　　　* headache〔'hɛd,ek〕*n.* 頭痛　　gone〔gɔn〕*adj.* 消失的
　　　　stop + V-ing 停止～　　cough〔kɔf〕*v.* 咳嗽
　　　　rest〔rɛst〕*v.* 休息　　*sth.* ***happen to sb.*** 某人發生某事
　　　　catch a cold 感冒　　hit〔hɪt〕*v.* 撞到 (三態同形)

22. (**B**) M：What do you like to do at the beach?

　　　　W：I like to play volleyball or lie in the sun.

　　　　M：How about swimming?

　　　　W：Oh. I never learned how.

　　　　Question：What can the girl do at the beach?

　　　　A. She can swim.

　　　　B. She can play volleyball.

　　　　C. She can snorkel.

　　　* beach〔bitʃ〕*n.* 海灘　　volleyball〔'vɑlɪ,bɔl〕*n.* 排球
　　　　lie〔laɪ〕*v.* 躺　　***in the sun*** 在太陽下
　　　　How about + V-ing? ～如何？
　　　　swim〔swɪm〕*v.* 游泳　　snorkel〔'snɔrkl̩〕*v.* 浮潛

23. (**A**) M：How would you like it cut?

W：I'd like it about shoulder-length.

M：Do you want me to add some curls?

W：No, thanks. I like it straight.

Question：Where did this conversation take place?

A. In a beauty salon.　　B. In a dress shop.

C. In a kitchen.

* cut〔kʌt〕v. 剪（頭髮）　　shoulder〔'ʃoldɚ〕n. 肩膀

length〔lɛŋθ〕n. 長度　　add〔æd〕v. 添加

curl〔kɝl〕n. 捲髮　　straight〔stret〕adj. 直的

conversation〔ˏkɑnvɚ'seʃən〕n. 對話

take place 發生　　*beauty salon* 美容院（= *beauty shop*）

dress〔drɛs〕n. 服裝

24. (**C**) W：Excuse me, am I allowed to smoke here?

M：I'm sorry, but there's no smoking or eating in

the theater.

W：That's O.K. I'll just go outside.

Question：What does the woman want to do?

A. Take a walk.　　B. Eat a snack.

C. Have a cigarette.

* allow〔ə'laʊ〕v. 允許

smoke〔smok〕v. 抽煙（= *have a cigarette*）

theater〔'θiətɚ〕n. 劇場；電影院

outside〔'aʊt'saɪd〕adv. 到外面　　*take a walk* 散步

snack〔snæk〕n. 點心　　cigarette〔'sɪgəˏrɛt〕n. 香煙

25. (**B**) M: Does this shirt go with these pants?

W: No. They don't match at all.

M: How about this one?

W: That looks much better.

Question: What does the girl say about the second shirt?

A. It is sold with the pants.

B. It matches the pants.

C. It doesn't go with the first shirt.

* shirt〔ʃɜt〕*n.* 襯衫　　***go with*** 相配 (= *match*〔mætʃ〕)
pants〔pænts〕*n. pl.* 褲子　　***not…at all*** 一點也不
How about~? 那~呢？　　look〔lʊk〕*v.* 看起來

26. (**B**) W: Can I help you?

M: Well, I'm actually looking for the bookstore.

W: Oh. That's on the fourth floor. You can take that escalator over there.

M: Thank you.

Question: Where did this conversation probably take place?

A. In a street market.　　B. In a shopping mall.

C. In a bookstore.

* actually〔'æktʃʊəlɪ〕*adv.* 事實上　　***look for*** 尋找
bookstore〔'bʊk,stor〕*n.* 書店　　floor〔flor〕*n.* 樓層
escalator〔'ɛskə,letə〕*n.* 手扶梯　　***over there*** 在那裡
probably〔'prɑbəblɪ〕*adv.* 可能
street〔strit〕*adj.* 街上的　　market〔'mɑrkɪt〕*n.* 市場
shopping mall 購物中心

27. (**C**) W：Excuse me, do you know when the next bus
        will come?

    M：Not exactly, but they come every ten minutes.

    W：How long have you been waiting?

    M：About five minutes.

    Question：How long will the girl have to wait for
            the bus?

    A. At least ten minutes.

    B. One minute.

    C. Less than five minutes.

    * *excuse me* 對不起   exactly〔ɪg'zæktlɪ〕*adv.* 確切地
       not exactly 不完全（知道）
       every ten minutes 每隔十分鐘
       How long~? ~多久？
       at least 至少   *less than* 少於

28. (**C**) W：When do you like to jog?

    M：I usually go jogging in the morning.

    W：Did you go jogging this morning?

    M：No, I didn't. I slept late today.

    Question：Why didn't the boy go jogging this morning?

    A. He stayed up studying last night and was too tired.

    B. He doesn't like to jog in the morning.

    C. He was sleeping this morning.

    * jog〔dʒɑg〕*v.* 慢跑
       I slept late today. 我今天很晚起床。   *stay up* 熬夜

29. (**C**)　W：You look different today.

　　　　　M：That's probably because I'm not wearing my glasses.

　　　　　W：What happened to them?

　　　　　M：Nothing.　I got contact lenses yesterday.

　　　　Question：What do we know about the boy?

　　　　A.　He lost his glasses.

　　　　B.　His eyesight is much better now.

　　　　C.　He wears contacts instead of glasses.

　　　　* different〔'dɪfərənt〕*adj.* 不同的　　wear〔wɛr〕*v.* 戴
　　　　　glasses〔'glæsɪz〕*n. pl.* 眼鏡　　get〔gɛt〕*v.* 買
　　　　　contact〔'kɑntækt〕*adj.* 接觸的　　lens〔lɛnz〕*n.* 鏡片
　　　　　contact lenses 隱形眼鏡（= *contacts*）
　　　　　lose〔luz〕*v.* 遺失　　eyesight〔'aɪ,saɪt〕*n.* 視力
　　　　　instead of 而不是

30. (**B**)　M：How did you do on the math test?

　　　　　W：Not so good.　In fact, I failed.

　　　　　M：I'm sorry to hear that.　Maybe I can help you.

　　　　　W：That would be great.　Let's meet at the library after
　　　　　　　school.

　　　　Question：What will the boy do?

　　　　A.　Help the girl find the library.

　　　　B.　Give the girl some math tips.

　　　　C.　Listen to the girl's excuses.

　　　　* ***in fact*** 事實上　　fail〔fel〕*v.*（考試）不及格
　　　　　meet〔mit〕*v.* 碰面　　library〔'laɪ,brɛrɪ〕*n.* 圖書館
　　　　　after school 放學後　　tip〔tɪp〕*n.* 秘訣
　　　　　listen to 聽　　excuse〔ɪk'skjus〕*n.* 藉口

全民英語能力分級檢定測驗

初級測驗⑤

　　本測驗分三部份，全為三選一之選擇題，每部份各 10 題，共 30 題，作答時間約 20 分鐘。

第一部份：看圖辨義

　　　　　本部份共 10 題，試題冊上每題有一個圖片，請聽錄音機播出一個相關的問題，與 A、B、C 三個英語敘述後，選一個與所看到圖片最相符的答案，並在答案紙上相對的圓圈內塗黑作答。每題播出一遍，問題及選項均不印在試題冊上。

例：（看）

NT$80　　NT$50

（聽）

Look at the picture.　How much is the hamburger?

　A. It's eighty dollars.
　B. It's fifty-five dollars.
　C. It's eighteen dollars.

正確答案為 A

A. Questions 1-2

B. Question 3

C. **Questions 4-5**

D. **Question 6**

請 翻 頁 ◖◻⟹

E. **Question 7**

F. **Question 8**

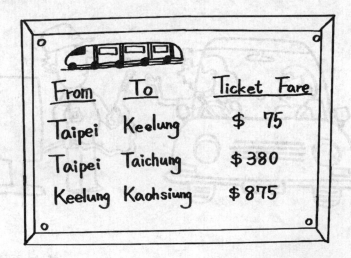

G. <u>Question 9</u>

H. <u>Question 10</u>

請翻頁 ⟹

第二部份： 問答

本部份共10題，每題錄音機會播出一個問句或直述句，每題播出一次，聽後請從試題冊上A、B、C三個選項中，選出一個最適合的回答或回應，並在答案紙上塗黑作答。

例：

（聽） Good morning, Kevin. How are you?

（看） A. I'm fine, thank you.
B. I'm in the living room.
C. My name is Kevin.

正確答案爲 A

11. A. That's kind of you, but my brother is going to meet me.
B. Oh, don't bother. I'll take a taxi to the station.
C. My train departs at 6:00.

12. A. No, neither did I.
B. No, I didn't. Did you?
C. No, I finished. Didn't you?

13. A. They live in
       apartment 4B.
    B. It's on the third floor,
       next to the shoes.
    C. I'm sorry. It's out of
       order now.

14. A. I'm fine, thank you.
    B. I came in second.
    C. Thank you. Good
       luck to you, too.

15. A. What's wrong with
       them?
    B. That will be $2300.
    C. You can try them on
       over there.

16. A. He did? That's
       wonderful.
    B. Better luck next time.
    C. I'm not surprised.
       He never studies.

17. A. Yes, it's my phone.
    B. It was someone for
       Dad.
    C. It's for you.

18. A. I had a wonderful
       time.
    B. Much better, thanks.
    C. See you soon.

19. A. The seafood platter
       is very good.
    B. I'd like to, but I have
       other plans.
    C. The French place on
       Park Street is good.

20. A. I wish I can go
       shopping.
    B. I will buy my father
       a new car.
    C. I would take a
       vacation.

請 翻 頁 ▐◻⟹

第三部份： 簡短對話

本部份共 10 題，每題錄音機會播出一段對話及一個相關的問題，每題播出兩次，聽後請從試題冊上 A、B、C 三個選項中，選出一個最適合的回答，並在答案紙上塗黑作答。

例：

（聽）(Woman) Good afternoon, ...Mr. Davis?

(Man) Yes. I have an appointment with Dr. Sanders at two o'clock. My son Tommy has a fever.

(Woman) Oh, that's too bad. Well, please have a seat, Mr. Davis. Dr. Sanders will be right with you.

Question: Where did this conversation take place?

（看）A. In a post office.

B. In a restaurant.

C. In a doctor's office.

正確答案爲 C

21. A. They are both fast runners.

B. They are members of different classes.

C. The woman's team is better than the man's team.

22. A. Forty-five.

B. Four.

C. None. They will take the test again.

23. A. They will go to a pizza restaurant.
    B. They will make a pizza at home.
    C. They will have a pizza delivered.

24. A. They will throw a surprise party for his mother.
    B. They will take his mother out to a nice restaurant.
    C. They will have a birthday party at home.

25. A. His mother thinks dogs are too cute.
    B. His mother likes dogs, but he doesn't.
    C. He likes dogs, but his mother doesn't.

26. A. Peter and the man should look at Peter's book.
    B. Peter should give the man his book.
    C. The man should not have forgotten his book.

27. A. A taxi ran through a puddle next to him.
    B. He was hit by a taxi.
    C. He fell into a puddle.

28. A. She is going to buy a new car.
    B. The car is being repaired.
    C. She is going to the bus station, not the school.

29. A. It is next to the post office.
    B. Through the park.
    C. It is a white building.

30. A. She has recovered from her injuries.
    B. She had an accident two days ago.
    C. She is a terrible driver.

請 翻 頁 ⃞⟹

初級英語聽力檢定⑤詳解

第一部份

For questions number 1 and 2, please look at picture A.

1. (**A**) What are Tracy's plans for this weekend?
   A. She will go to the dentist.
   B. She will have coffee with Helen.
   C. She has no plans.

   * plan (plæn) *n.* 計劃　weekend ('wik'ɛnd) *n.* 週末
   dentist ('dɛntɪst) *n.* 牙醫　coffee ('kɔfɪ) *n.* 咖啡

2. (**B**) Please look at picture A again. When will Tracy go to see the movie?
   A. On April 12th.
   B. On April 13th.
   C. On April 14th.

   * movie ('muvɪ) *n.* 電影

For question number 3, please look at picture B.

3. (**C**) When does the English class start?
   A. At seven fifty.
   B. At eight o'clock.
   C. At eight ten.

   * class (klæs) *n.* (一節) 課
   start (stɑrt) *v.* 開始 (= *begin*)

For questions number 4 and 5, please look at picture C.

4. (**A**) How's the weather?

    A. It's rainy and windy.

    B. It's hot and sunny.

    C. It's cool and foggy.

    * weather (ˈwɛðɚ) *n.* 天氣　　rainy (ˈrenɪ) *adj.* 下雨的

    windy (ˈwɪndɪ) *adj.* 風大的

    sunny (ˈsʌnɪ) *adj.* 陽光充足的；天氣晴朗的

    cool (kul) *adj.* 涼爽的　　foggy (ˈfɑgɪ) *adj.* 有霧的

5. (**A**) Please look at picture C again. What did the boy step in?

    A. A puddle.

    B. A rain shower.

    C. His shoe is wet.

    * step (stɛp) *v.* 踏 (進)　　puddle (ˈpʌdl̩) *n.* 水坑

    shower (ˈʃauɚ) *n.* 陣雨　　shoe (ʃu) *n.* 鞋子

    wet (wɛt) *adj.* 濕的

For question number 6, please look at picture D.

6. (**C**) What will the attendant do?

    A. Buy some gas.

    B. Ask for directions.

    C. Put gas in the car.

    * attendant (əˈtɛndənt) *n.* 服務人員

    gas (gæs) *n.* 汽油　　direction (dəˈrɛkʃən) *n.* 方向

    ask for directions 問路　　put (put) *v.* 將…灌入 < *in* >

For question number 7, please look at picture E.

7. (**C**) The customer wants to go to the next movie with her three children. How much will she pay?

    A. $8 each.   B. $30.

    C. $45.

    * customer〔'kʌstəmə〕n. 顧客
      go to the next movie 看下一場電影   pay〔pe〕v. 付費
      each〔itʃ〕*adv.* 每一個   adult〔ə'dʌlt〕n. 大人
      一個大人（$15）＋三個小孩（$10×3）＝$45

For question number 8, please look at picture F.

8. (**B**) What is the fare from Taipei to Kaohsiung?

    A. Seventy-five dollars.   B. We don't know.

    C. Eight hundred and seventy-five dollars.

    * fare〔fɛr〕n. 車費   ***from…to~*** 從…到~
      Kaohsiung 高雄   ***Keelung*** 基隆   ***Taichung*** 台中

For question number 9, please look at picture G.

9. (**A**) If you are in the park and are facing the school, where will the bank be?

    A. On your right.   B. On your left.

    C. Behind you.

    * face〔fes〕v. 面向   bank〔bæŋk〕n. 銀行
      right〔raɪt〕n. 右邊（↔ left〔lɛft〕左邊）
      on one's right 在某人的右邊（↔ *on one's left*）
      behind〔bɪ'haɪnd〕*prep.* 在…的背後
      restaurant〔'rɛstərənt〕n. 餐廳

For question number 10, please look at picture H.

10. (**B**) Why is the girl crying?

      A. She fell from the tree.

      B. She is frightened.

      C. She does not like the boy.

      * fall〔fɔl〕v. 跌落 (三態變化為：fall-fell-fallen)

        tree〔tri〕n. 樹   frightened〔'fraɪtṇd〕adj. 害怕的

第二部份

11. (**A**) What time will you arrive tomorrow? I'll pick you up at the station.

      A. That's kind of you, but my brother is going to meet me.

      B. Oh, don't bother. I'll take a taxi to the station.

      C. My train departs at 6:00.

      * arrive〔ə'raɪv〕v. 到達   ***pick sb. up*** 開車接某人

        station〔'steʃən〕n. 車站   kind〔kaɪnd〕adj. 好心的

        meet〔mit〕v. 迎接   bother〔'baðɚ〕v. 麻煩；費心

        depart〔dɪ'pɑrt〕v. 出發

12. (**B**) You finished the homework, didn't you?

      A. No, neither did I.

      B. No, I didn't. Did you?

      C. No, I finished. Didn't you?

      * finish〔'fɪnɪʃ〕v. 完成   homework〔'hom‚wɝk〕n. 功課

        neither〔'niðɚ〕adv. 也不

13. (**B**) Can you tell me where the men's department is?

    A. They live in apartment 4B.

    B. It's on the third floor, next to the shoes.

    C. I'm sorry. It's out of order now.

    * department〔dɪ'partmənt〕*n.* 部門
    men's department 男裝部
    apartment〔ə'partmənt〕*n.* 公寓   floor〔flor〕*n.* 樓層
    next to 在…隔壁   sorry〔'sɔrɪ〕*adj.* 抱歉的
    out of order 故障

14. (**B**) How did you do in the speech contest?

    A. I'm fine, thank you.

    B. I came in second.

    C. Thank you. Good luck to you, too.

    * speech〔spitʃ〕*n.* 演講   contest〔'kantɛst〕*n.* 比賽
    come in （比賽）得名次
    come in second （比賽）得第二名   luck〔lʌk〕*n.* 運氣
    Good luck to you, too. 也祝你好運。

15. (**A**) I'd like to return these shoes.

    A. What's wrong with them?

    B. That will be $2300.

    C. You can try them on over there.

    * ***would like to V.*** 想要～   return〔rɪ'tɝn〕*v.* 退回
    What's wrong with～? ～怎麼了？（＝ *What's the matter*
    with～? ）   ***try on*** 試穿   ***over there*** 在那裡

16. (**C**) I hear that John failed the exam.

　　A. He did?　That's wonderful.

　　B. Better luck next time.

　　C. I'm not surprised.　He never studies.

　　* hear〔hɪr〕v. 聽說　　fail〔fel〕v.（考試）不及格

　　　exam〔ɪg'zæm〕n. 考試

　　　wonderful〔'wʌndəfəl〕adj. 很棒的

　　　Better luck next time. 祝你下次運氣好一點。

　　　（對方這次考試或比賽等失敗時用）

　　　surprised〔sə'praɪzd〕adj. 感到驚訝的

　　　study〔'stʌdɪ〕v. 唸書

17. (**B**) Who was on the phone?

　　A. Yes, it's my phone.

　　B. It was someone for Dad.

　　C. It's for you.

　　* phone〔fon〕n. 電話

　　　Who was on the phone? 是誰打電話來的？

18. (**B**) Welcome back.　How do you feel?

　　A. I had a wonderful time.

　　B. Much better, thanks.

　　C. See you soon.

　　* ***Welcome back.*** 歡迎回來。

　　　have a wonderful time 玩得很愉快

　　　better〔'bɛtə〕adj. 健康狀況有所好轉的（well 的比較級）

　　　See you soon. 再見。

19. (**C**) Can you recommend a good restaurant?
　　A. The seafood platter is very good.
　　B. I'd like to, but I have other plans.
　　C. The French place on Park Street is good.

　　* recommend〔‚rɛkə'mɛnd〕v. 推薦
　　　seafood〔'si‚fud〕n. 海鮮
　　　platter〔'plætə〕n. 大淺盤
　　　seafood platter 海鮮拼盤
　　　French〔frɛntʃ〕adj. 法國的
　　　place〔ples〕n. (有特定用途的)場所 (這裡是指「餐廳」)

20. (**C**) What would you do if you won the lottery?
　　A. I wish I can go shopping.
　　B. I will buy my father a new car.
　　C. I would take a vacation.

　　* win〔wɪn〕v. 贏 (三態變化為：win-won-won)
　　　lottery〔'lɑtərɪ〕n. 彩券；樂透
　　　What would you do if you won the lottery? 如果你中了
　　　　樂透，你會做什麼？(此為「與現在事實相反」的假設語氣
　　　　用法，故答句須用假設語氣，A. 須改為 I wish I could go
　　　　shopping. B. 須改為 I would buy my father a new car.
　　　　才能選。)
　　　wish〔wɪʃ〕v. 但願；希望 (引導假設語氣的子句)
　　　go shopping 去購物
　　　vacation〔ve'keʃən〕n. 假期
　　　take a vacation 去渡假

第三部份

21. (**B**) M: Are you going to compete in any of the School Sports Day events?

W: Yes, I'm on the relay race team. I think we have a good chance of winning because we have some fast runners in our class.

M: Don't be so sure. There are some good runners in my class, too.

W: Well, may the best team win.

Question : What do we know about the two speakers?

A. They are both fast runners.

B. They are members of different classes.

C. The woman's team is better than the man's team.

* compete〔kəm'pit〕v. 比賽
  sports〔sports〕adj. 運動的
  sports day （學校）運動會日
  event〔ɪ'vɛnt〕n. （比賽）項目
  relay〔'rile〕n. 接力賽
  race〔res〕n. 賽跑　　team〔tim〕n. 隊
  chance〔tʃæns〕n. 機會；可能性
  runner〔'rʌnɚ〕n. 賽跑者　　sure〔ʃur〕adj. 確信的
  may〔me〕v. 祝；願（表示希望、祝願等）
  speaker〔'spikɚ〕n. 說話者
  member〔'mɛmbɚ〕n. 成員
  different〔'dɪfərənt〕adj. 不同的

22. (**B**) M: How did your students do on the exam?

W: Pretty good. Four out of five passed.

M: What about the one who didn't?

W: He'll have to take the test again.

Question : How many students passed the exam?

A. Forty-five.

B. Four.

C. None. They will take the test again.

* pretty〔'prɪtɪ〕*adv.* 相當　***out of*** 從（某個數目）中
four out of five 五個當中有四個
pass〔pæs〕*v.*（考試）及格；通過
What about~? 那~呢？　***have to V.*** 必須~

23. (**C**) W: What do you want to do for dinner?

M: I don't feel like going out.

W: Then why don't we order a pizza?

Question : What will they do for dinner?

A. They will go to a pizza restaurant.

B. They will make a pizza at home.

C. They will have a pizza delivered.

* ***feel like*** + ***V-ing*** 想要~　***go out*** 外出
order〔'ɔrdɚ〕*v.* 點（餐）　pizza〔'pitsə〕*n.* 披薩
make〔mek〕*v.* 做
have〔hæv〕*v.* 要（「have + 受詞 + p.p.」表「被動」）
deliver〔dɪ'lɪvɚ〕*v.* 遞送

24. (**C**) W: What a beautiful cake! What's the occasion?

M: Today is my mother's birthday, and we're having a party tonight.

W: Is it a surprise party?

M: I hope not! Mom is supposed to cook the dinner.

Question : What will the man's family do tonight?

A. They will throw a surprise party for his mother.

B. They will take his mother out to a nice restaurant.

C. They will have a birthday party at home.

* cake〔kek〕n. 蛋糕　　occasion〔əˈkeʒən〕n. 重大場合
  have a party 舉行派對（= *throw a party*）
  surprise party 令人驚喜、沒有事先通知的派對
  be supposed to V. 應該（= *should V.*）
  cook〔kʊk〕v. 煮　　***take sb. out*** 帶某人出去

25. (**C**) M: I wish I could get a dog.

W: Why don't you?

M: My mother won't allow it.

W: Doesn't she like dogs?

M: No. She says they're cute but too much trouble.

Question : Why can't the man have a dog?

A. His mother thinks dogs are too cute.

B. His mother likes dogs, but he doesn't.

C. He likes dogs, but his mother doesn't.

* get〔gɛt〕v. 得到　　allow〔əˈlaʊ〕v. 准許
  cute〔kjut〕adj. 可愛的　　trouble〔ˈtrʌbl̩〕n. 麻煩

26. (**A**) W: Class, please open your books to page 47.

M: I'm sorry, teacher, but I forgot to bring my book.

W: Then you'll have to share with Peter.

Question : What does the woman mean?

A. Peter and the man should look at Peter's book.

B. Peter should give the man his book.

C. The man should not have forgotten his book.

* class〔klæs〕n. 全班同學　　forget〔fəˋgɛt〕v. 忘記
then〔ðɛn〕adv. 那麼　　share〔ʃɛr〕v. 共同使用
mean〔min〕v. 意思是　　*look at* 看
should not have + *p.p.* 當初不應該 (表示過去不該做而做)

27. (**A**) W: You're all wet! Is it raining?

M: Only a little.

W: Then what happened?

M: I was splashed by a taxi when it went through a puddle.

Question : What happened to the man?

A. A taxi ran through a puddle next to him.

B. He was hit by a taxi.

C. He fell into a puddle.

* *a little* 一點　　happen〔ˋhæpən〕v. 發生
splash〔splæʃ〕v. 濺；潑
go through 經過 (= *run through*)
puddle〔ˋpʌdḷ〕n. 水坑
sth. *happen to* *sb.* 某人發生某事　　hit〔hɪt〕v. 撞

28. (**B**) M: Can you give me a ride to school today?

W: I'm sorry, the car is in the shop.

M: That's all right. I'll take a bus.

Question : Why doesn't the woman drive the man to school?

A. She is going to buy a new car.

B. The car is being repaired.

C. She is going to the bus station, not the school.

* ride〔raɪd〕*n.* 乘坐　　***give sb. a ride*** 讓某人搭便車

shop〔ʃɑp〕*n.* 工廠　　***all right*** 沒關係

drive〔draɪv〕*v.* 開車送（人）

repair〔rɪ'pɛr〕*v.* 修理　　***bus station*** 公車站

29. (**B**) W: Excuse me, do you know where the bank is?

M: Yes, it's next to the post office.

W: Where's that?

M: It's on the other side of the park. See? It's that white building over there.

Question : How will the woman get to the bank?

A. It is next to the post office.

B. Through the park.

C. It is a white building.

* ***excuse me*** 對不起　　bank〔bæŋk〕*n.* 銀行

post office 郵局　　side〔saɪd〕*n.* 邊

see〔si〕*v.* 你看；瞧　　building〔'bɪldɪŋ〕*n.* 建築物

get to 到達　　through〔θru〕*prep.* 穿過

30. (**A**) M: Long time no see. Where have you been?

W: Actually, I was in the hospital for a couple of days.

M: What happened?

W: Oh, I had a car accident, but I'm all right now.

Question : What do we know about the woman?

A. She has recovered from her injuries.

B. She had an accident two days ago.

C. She is a terrible driver.

* ***Long time no see.*** 好久不見。
  actually〔'æktʃʋəlɪ〕*adv.* 實際上（= *in fact* ）
  hospital〔'hɑspɪtḷ〕*n.* 醫院　　couple〔'kʌpḷ〕*n.* 兩個
  a couple of 幾個（= *several* ）
  accident〔'æksədənt〕*n.* 意外；車禍
  all right （健康）良好的
  recover〔rɪ'kʌvɚ〕*v.* 恢復健康 <*from* >
  injury〔'ɪndʒərɪ〕*n.* 傷害
  terrible〔'tɛrəbḷ〕*adj.* 糟糕的
  driver〔'draɪvɚ〕*n.* 駕駛

全民英語能力分級檢定測驗
初級測驗⑥

　　本測驗分三部份，全為三選一之選擇題，每部份各 10 題，共 30 題，作答時間約 20 分鐘。

第一部份：看圖辨義

　　　　本部份共 10 題，試題冊上每題有一個圖片，請聽錄音機播出一個相關的問題，與 A、B、C 三個英語敘述後，選一個與所看到圖片最相符的答案，並在答案紙上相對的圓圈內塗黑作答。每題播出一遍，問題及選項均不印在試題冊上。

例：（看）

NT$80　　NT$50

（聽）

Look at the picture.　How much is the hamburger?

　　A. It's eighty dollars.
　　B. It's fifty-five dollars.
　　C. It's eighteen dollars.

正確答案為 A

A. <u>Questions 1-2</u>

B. <u>Question 3</u>

C. <u>Questions 4-5</u>

D. <u>Question 6</u>

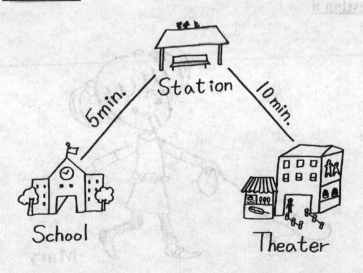

請翻頁 ▯▭▻

E. **Question 7**

F. **Question 8**

Mary

G. **Question 9**

H. **Question 10**

請翻頁 ▯▯▯⟹

第二部份： 問答

本部份共 10 題，每題錄音機會播出一個問句或直述句，
每題播出一次，聽後請從試題冊上 A、B、C 三個選項
中，選出一個最適合的回答或回應，並在答案紙上塗黑
作答。

例：

（聽）　Good morning, Kevin.　How are you?

（看）　A.　I'm fine, thank you.
　　　　B.　I'm in the living room.
　　　　C.　My name is Kevin.

　　　　正確答案爲 A

11. A. Say hello to her for
       me.
    B. I'd like to, but I can't.
    C. How long have you
       known each other?

12. A. Yes, it might.
    B. I'm not supposed to.
    C. Then we can't go on
       a picnic.

13. A. It was in the kitchen.
    B. It comes from Italy.
    C. It's a little salty.

14. A. Have you been
       waiting long?
    B. Sorry to make you
       wait so long.
    C. Let's wait a little
       while longer.

15. A. My name is Peter.
    B. No, I don't have one.
    C. Yes, he's very nice.

16. A. Thank you. That's very kind of you.
    B. Sorry. I'll sit down right away.
    C. I'm sorry, but this seat is taken.

17. A. Is he all right?
    B. Can you cut mine, too?
    C. Yes, it does look shorter.

18. A. Of course I did. I got an A.
    B. Of course not. I have never failed a test.
    C. Of course you did. Don't worry.

19. A. Yes, a little milk, please.
    B. I'd prefer water.
    C. Of course. Here you are.

20. A. Yes, I am.
    B. There is bus to Taichung every half hour.
    C. Yes. It leaves in five minutes.

請 翻 頁 ⬅⟹

第三部份：簡短對話

本部份共 10 題，每題錄音機會播出一段對話及一個相關的問題，每題播出兩次，聽後請從試題冊上 A、B、C 三個選項中，選出一個最適合的回答，並在答案紙上塗黑作答。

例：

（聽）(Woman) Good afternoon, ...Mr. Davis?

(Man) Yes. I have an appointment with Dr. Sanders at two o'clock. My son Tommy has a fever.

(Woman) Oh, that's too bad. Well, please have a seat, Mr. Davis. Dr. Sanders will be right with you.

Question: Where did this conversation take place?

（看）A. In a post office.

B. In a restaurant.

C. In a doctor's office.

正確答案為 C

21. A. A trip to a local museum.

B. A bus to her hotel.

C. The entrance fee to the national park.

22. A. He will not join the club.

B. He will borrow some money from the woman.

C. He will let the woman treat him.

23. A. Try black shoes in a
       larger size.
    B. Try larger brown shoes.
    C. Buy black shoes in the
       same size.

24. A. He carried the box to
       the door.
    B. He opened the door.
    C. He helped the woman
       carry the box.

25. A. Lasagna is more
       special than spaghetti.
    B. He wants to taste the
       lasagna before he
       orders it.
    C. He will order the
       lasagna.

26. A. It is going too fast to
       stop.
    B. It does not make local
       stops.
    C. The man got on the
       wrong train.

27. A. Judy Brown is a new
       student at Peter's
       school.
    B. Judy Brown is Peter's
       aunt.
    C. Peter and Wendy are
       classmates.

28. A. It started too late.
    B. The show was sold out.
    C. It started at 9:00.

29. A. Call him when she is
       finished with the notes.
    B. Keep the notes because
       he doesn't need them.
    C. Feel free to call him
       with questions.

30. A. He would rather go on
       a picnic with his
       relatives.
    B. He would rather go to
       the mountains.
    C. He would rather spend
       time with his relatives.

請 翻 頁 ◀▯⟹

初級英語聽力檢定⑥詳解

第一部份

For questions number 1 and 2, please look at picture A.

1. (**C**) Who is first in line?
   A. There are three people in line.
   B. They will take the first bus.
   C. The businessman.

   * line〔laɪn〕*n.* 行列
     businessman〔'bɪznɪsmən, 'bɪznɪs,mæn〕*n.* 商人
     bus stop 公車站

2. (**A**) Please look at picture A again. What is the third person in line wearing?
   A. Sunglasses.
   B. A suit.
   C. A skirt.

   * wear〔wɛr〕*v.* 戴（眼鏡）；穿（衣服）
     sunglasses〔'sʌn,glæsɪz〕*n. pl.* 太陽眼鏡
     suit〔sut〕*n.* 西裝　　skirt〔skɝt〕*n.* 裙子

For question number 3, please look at picture B.

3. (**B**) If you have NT$120, what can you buy?

      A. Four sandwiches.   B. Two colas.

      C. One sandwich and one cola.

      * *NT$* 新台幣 (= *New Taiwan dollars*)

      sandwich〔'sændwɪtʃ〕*n.* 三明治   cola〔'kolə〕*n.* 可樂

For questions number 4 and 5, please look at picture C.

4. (**B**) How many people are there on the beach?

      A. They're having a good time there.

      B. There are two children and two adults on the beach.

      C. They get there by car.

      * beach〔bitʃ〕*n.* 海灘   *have a good time* 玩得高興

      adult〔ə'dʌlt〕*n.* 成人   *get there* 到達那裡

      by car 搭乘汽車

5. (**B**) Please look at picture C again. What are the children going to do?

      A. Drive to the beach in the car.

      B. Play in the waves.

      C. Have a picnic on the beach.

      * drive〔draɪv〕*v.* 開車   wave〔wev〕*n.* 波浪

      the waves 海   picnic〔'pɪknɪk〕*n.* 野餐

      have a picnic 去野餐 (= *go on a picnic*)

For question number 6, please look at picture D.

6. (**B**) The movie starts at quarter after eight. When is the
latest time we should leave the school?
A. Seven forty-five.
B. Eight o'clock.
C. Eight ten.

* start〔start〕*v.* 開始
quarter〔'kwɔrtɚ〕*n.* 一刻鐘;十五分
at (a) quarter after eight 在八點十五分
latest〔'letɪst〕*adj.* 最遲的   leave〔liv〕*v.* 離開
theater〔'θiətɚ〕*n.* 電影院

For question number 7, please look at picture E.

7. (**C**) What is the student doing?
A. He is wearing a raincoat.
B. He is walking to school in the rain.
C. He is crossing the street.

* raincoat〔'ren͵kot〕*n.* 雨衣   cross〔krɔs〕*v.* 穿越

For question number 8, please look at picture F.

8. (**B**) What is Mary holding?
A. She is walking her dog.
B. She has a leash in her hand.
C. The dog is pulling Mary.

* hold〔hold〕*v.* 握著   walk〔wɔk〕*v.* 遛(狗)
leash〔liʃ〕*n.* 狗鍊   pull〔pul〕*v.* 拉

For question number 9, please look at picture G.

9. (**C**) Where are they playing?

    A. They are playing cards.

    B. A deck of cards.

    C. On the table.

    * cards〔kɑrdz〕*n. pl.* 紙牌遊戲　　***play cards*** 玩撲克牌

    deck〔dɛk〕*n.* (紙牌的) 一副

For question number 10, please look at picture H.

10. (**A**) What are the girls doing?

    A. They are cheering.

    B. There are three runners.

    C. They are running a race.

    * cheer〔tʃɪr〕*v.* 歡呼　　runner〔'rʌnɚ〕*n.* 賽跑者

    race〔res〕*n.* 賽跑　　***run a race*** 賽跑

第二部份

11. (**A**) I'm going to meet my sister at the movies.

    A. Say hello to her for me.

    B. I'd like to, but I can't.

    C. How long have you known each other?

    * meet〔mit〕*v.* 與 (某人) 碰面

    movie〔'muvɪ〕*n.* 電影院

    say hello to *sb.* 向某人問好

    How long~? ～多久 (時間) ?

    each other 彼此

12. (**A**) Is it supposed to rain tomorrow?

    A. Yes, it might.

    B. I'm not supposed to.

    C. Then we can't go on a picnic.

    * suppose〔səˈpoz〕v. 認為
    be supposed to V. 應該

13. (**C**) How do you find the spaghetti?

    A. It was in the kitchen.

    B. It comes from Italy.

    C. It's a little salty.

    * find〔faɪnd〕v. 覺得　　spaghetti〔spəˈgɛtɪ〕n. 義大利麵
    come from 源自　　Italy〔ˈɪtl̩ɪ〕n. 義大利
    a little 有點　　salty〔ˈsɔltɪ〕adj. 鹹的

14. (**B**) Finally! I've been waiting for you for an hour!

    A. Have you been waiting long?

    B. Sorry to make you wait so long.

    C. Let's wait a little while longer.

    * finally〔ˈfaɪnl̩ɪ〕adv. 最後；終於
    wait for 等待　　while〔hwaɪl〕n. 一會兒

15. (**C**) Have you met our new classmate, Tim?

    A. My name is Peter.

    B. No, I don't have one.

    C. Yes, he's very nice.

    * meet〔mit〕v. 認識　　classmate〔ˈklæs,met〕n. 同學

16. (**B**) Please remain seated until the plane stops.

    A. Thank you. That's very kind of you.

    B. Sorry. I'll sit down right away.

    C. I'm sorry, but this seat is taken.

    * remain〔rɪ'men〕v. 保持　　seated〔'sitɪd〕adj. 就座的
    until〔ən'tɪl〕conj. 直到　　plane〔plen〕n. 飛機
    kind〔kaɪnd〕adj. 好心的　　*sit down* 坐下
    right away 馬上　　seat〔sit〕n. 座位
    take〔tek〕v. 佔據

17. (**C**) I think John had his hair cut.

    A. Is he all right?

    B. Can you cut mine, too?

    C. Yes, it does look shorter.

    * hair〔hɛr〕n. 頭髮　　cut〔kʌt〕n. 剪（三態同形）
    have one's hair cut 某人剪頭髮
    all right （健康）良好的

18. (**A**) You passed the test, didn't you?

    A. Of course I did. I got an A.

    B. Of course not. I have never failed a test.

    C. Of course you did. Don't worry.

    * pass〔pæs〕v. （考試）及格　　test〔tɛst〕n. 考試
    Of course. 當然。　　A （成績）優等
    Of course not. 當然不。　　fail〔fel〕v. （考試）不及格
    worry〔'wɝɪ〕v. 擔心

19. (**B**) Would you like a cup of tea?

    A. Yes, a little milk, please.

    B. I'd prefer water.

    C. Of course. Here you are.

    * ***would like*** 想要 (= *want*)

      tea〔ti〕*n.* 茶　　***a little*** 一些

      milk〔mɪlk〕*n.* 牛奶

      prefer〔prɪˈfɝ〕*v.* 比較喜歡

      Here you are. 你要的東西在這裡；拿去吧。

        (= *Here it is.* = *Here you go.*)

20. (**C**) Is this the bus to Taichung?

    A. Yes, I am.

    B. There is bus to Taichung every half hour.

    C. Yes. It leaves in five minutes.

    * ***Taichung*** 台中　　half〔hæf〕*adj.* 一半的

      every half hour 每半小時

      in five minutes 再過五分鐘

第三部份

21.(**B**) W: Can you tell me about your tour to Hawaii?

M: Of course. We offer a five-day tour that includes hotel, airfare, and three meals a day.

W: How about local transportation?

M: Transportation to and from the hotel in Hawaii by minibus is included.

Question : According to the travel agent, the woman will not have to pay for which of the following?

A. A trip to a local museum.

B. A bus to her hotel.

C. The entrance fee to the national park.

* tour〔tʊr〕*n.* 旅行（= *trip*）

Hawaii〔hə'waɪjə〕*n.* 夏威夷　　offer〔'ɔfɚ〕*v.* 提供

a five-day tour 五天四夜之旅　　include〔ɪn'klud〕*v.* 包括

hotel〔ho'tɛl〕*n.* 旅館　　airfare〔'ɛr,fɛr〕*n.* 飛機票價

meal〔mil〕*n.*（一）餐　　*How about ~ ?* 那麼 ~ 如何？

local〔'lokl̩〕*adj.* 當地的

transportation〔,trænspɚ'teʃən〕*n.* 交通運輸

to and from 來回

minibus〔'mɪnɪ,bʌs〕*n.* 迷你巴士；小型巴士

according to 根據　　travel〔'trævl̩〕*n.* 旅行

agent〔'edʒənt〕*n.* 代理人　　*travel agent* 旅遊代辦人

pay for 爲 ~ 付費　　following〔'faləwɪŋ〕*adj.* 下面的

museum〔mju'ziəm〕*n.* 博物館

entrance〔'ɛntrəns〕*n.* 進入　　fee〔fi〕*n.* 費用

entrance fee 入場費　　*national park* 國家公園

22. (**B**) W: Did you remember to bring some money for the club membership fee?

M: Oh, no! I forgot.

W: Don't worry. I can lend it to you.

M: Thanks. You're a real friend.

W: Don't mention it. After all, I don't want to join the club without you.

Question : What will the man do?

A. He will not join the club.

B. He will borrow some money from the woman.

C. He will let the woman treat him.

* remember 〔 rɪˋmɛmbɚ 〕 v. 記得

club 〔 klʌb 〕 n. 俱樂部；社團

membership 〔ˋmɛmbɚˏʃɪp 〕 n. 會員身分（或地位、資格）

membership fee 會員費   forget 〔 fɚˋgɛt 〕 v. 忘記

lend 〔 lɛnd 〕 v. 借（出）   real 〔ˋriəl 〕 adj. 眞正的

mention 〔ˋmɛnʃən 〕 v. 提到

Don't mention it. 不客氣。（ = *You are welcome.* ）

after all 畢竟   join 〔 dʒɔɪn 〕 v. 參加

without 〔 wɪðˋaut 〕 prep. 沒有

borrow 〔ˋbaro 〕 v. 借（入）

let 〔 lɛt 〕 v. 讓（三態同形）

treat 〔 trit 〕 v. 請客；款待

23. (**A**) M: How do the shoes fit?

W: Well, they're a little tight.

M: I'm afraid we don't have a larger size in brown.

W: How about in black?

M: I'll check.

Question : What does the woman want to do next?

A. Try black shoes in a larger size.

B. Try larger brown shoes.

C. Buy black shoes in the same size.

* shoe〔ʃu〕*n.* 鞋子   fit〔fɪt〕*v.* 合（腳）；合（身）
tight〔taɪt〕*adj.* 緊的   *I'm afraid (that)* 恐怕～
size〔saɪz〕*n.* 尺寸   brown〔braʊn〕*n.* 棕色
check〔tʃɛk〕*v.* 檢查；核對   next〔nɛkst〕*adv.* 接下來

24. (**B**) M: Do you want some help with that box?

W: That's O.K. It's not that heavy.

M: At least let me get the door for you.

W: Thanks.

Question : What did the man do?

A. He carried the box to the door.

B. He opened the door.

C. He helped the woman carry the box.

* box〔bɑks〕*n.* 箱子   *That's O.K.* 沒關係。
that〔ðæt〕*adv.* 那麼   heavy〔'hɛvɪ〕*adj.* 重的
at least 至少   *let me get the door for you* 讓我幫你開門
carry〔'kærɪ〕*v.* 搬；提   open〔'opən〕*v.* 打開

25. (**C**) M: How is the spaghetti here?

W: It's good, but the lasagna is our specialty.

M: In that case, I'll try it.

Question : What does the man mean?

A. Lasagna is more special than spaghetti.

B. He wants to taste the lasagna before he orders it.

C. He will order the lasagna.

* spaghetti〔spə'gɛtɪ〕n. 義大利麵
  lasagna〔lə'zɑnjə〕n. 義大利千層麵
  specialty〔'spɛʃəltɪ〕n. 招牌菜　　***in that case*** 既然那樣
  mean〔min〕v. 意思是　　special〔'spɛʃəl〕adj. 特別的
  taste〔test〕v. 品嚐　　order〔'ɔrdɚ〕v. 點（菜）

26. (**B**) M: Excuse me, does this train stop in Springfield?

W: No, this is an express.

M: How can I get to Springfield?

W: You can get off at the next stop and change to a
   train that makes local stops.

Question : Why won't the train stop at Springfield?

A. It is going too fast to stop.

B. It does not make local stops.

C. The man got on the wrong train.

* ***excuse me*** 對不起　　stop〔stap〕v. 停車　n. 停車站
  express〔ɪk'sprɛs〕n. 快車　　***get to*** 到達　　***get off*** 下車
  change〔tʃendʒ〕v. 換車　　***make a stop*** （火車等）停靠
  local〔'lokl〕adj.（公共交通工具）每站停的
  make a local stop 每站都停
  too…to V. 太…以致於不～　　***get on*** 上（車）

27. (**C**) W: Peter, do you remember my Aunt Judy?

　　　　M: Yes. It's nice to see you again, Mrs. Brown.

　　　　W: I'm taking Aunt Judy to see our school.

　　　　M: That's a great idea, Wendy.

　　　Question : Which of the following is true?

　　　A. Judy Brown is a new student at Peter's school.

　　　B. Judy Brown is Peter's aunt.

　　　C. Peter and Wendy are classmates.

　　* aunt〔 ænt 〕*n.* 阿姨；姑媽；伯母

　　　idea〔 aɪˈdiə 〕*n.* 主意　　true〔 tru 〕*adj.* 真實的；正確的

28. (**A**) M: Which movie do you want to see?

　　　　W: Let's see *Hero*.

　　　　M: But that one's already started, and the next show

　　　　　　isn't until 11:00.

　　　　W: That's too late. How about *Happy Times*?

　　　　M: Okay. That starts at 9:00.

　　　Question : Why didn't they see *Hero*?

　　　A. It started too late.　　　B. The show was sold out.

　　　C. It started at 9:00.

　　* hero〔ˈhɪro 〕*n.* 英雄　　start〔 stɑrt 〕*v.* 開始

　　　already〔 ɔlˈrɛdɪ 〕*adv.* 已經　　show〔 ʃo 〕*n.* 電影放映

　　　until〔 ənˈtɪl 〕*prep.* 直到　　late〔 let 〕*adj.* 晚的　*adv.* 晚

　　　times〔 taɪmz 〕*n. pl.* 時光

　　　okay〔ˈoˈke 〕*interj.* 好；沒問題 (= O.K.)

　　　sell out 賣完

29. (**C**) W: Thanks for lending me your notes.

M: It's no problem. What are friends for?

W: I'll give them back to you as soon as I'm finished copying them.

M: There's no rush. Give me a call if you have any questions.

Question : What does the man tell the woman to do?

A. Call him when she is finished with the notes.

B. Keep the notes because he doesn't need them.

C. Feel free to call him with questions.

* note〔not〕*n.* 筆記　problem〔'prɑbləm〕*n.* 問題

It's no problem. 不客氣。(= *No problem.*)

What are friends for? 朋友是做什麼的？；朋友就該

　　互相幫忙。

give back 歸還 (= *return*)

as soon as 一…就~

finished〔'fɪnɪʃt〕*adj.* 完成的

copy〔'kɑpɪ〕*v.* 抄寫　rush〔rʌʃ〕*n.* 匆忙

There's no rush. 不急。

give *sb.* **a call** 打電話給某人

question〔'kwɛstʃən〕*n.* 問題　keep〔kip〕*v.* 保有

free〔fri〕*adj.* 隨意的；不受約束的

30. (**C**) M: Where are you going this weekend?

W: I want to go on a picnic, so we'll probably go to the mountains.

M: That sounds like fun.

W: Would you like to join us?

M: I'd like to, but my relatives are in town this week and I want to spend some time with them.

Question : What does the man mean?

A. He would rather go on a picnic with his relatives.

B. He would rather go to the mountains.

C. He would rather spend time with his relatives.

* weekend (ˈwikˈɛnd) n. 週末
  go on a picnic 去野餐
  probably (ˈprɑbəblɪ) adv. 大概；或許
  mountain (ˈmauntn̩) n. 山
  go to the mountains 去山上
  sound like + N. 聽起來～
  fun (fʌn) n. 樂趣
  relative (ˈrɛlətɪv) n. 親戚
  in town 在城裡；在市中心
  would rather 寧願

心得筆記欄

全民英語能力分級檢定測驗
初級測驗 ⑦

　　本測驗分三部份，全為三選一之選擇題，每部份各 10 題，共 30 題，作答時間約 20 分鐘。

第一部份：看圖辨義

　　　　本部份共 10 題，試題冊上每題有一個圖片，請聽錄音機播出一個相關的問題，與 A、B、C 三個英語敘述後，選一個與所看到圖片最相符的答案，並在答案紙上相對的圓圈內塗黑作答。每題播出一遍，問題及選項均不印在試題冊上。

例：（看）

NT$80　　NT$50

（聽）

Look at the picture.　How much is the hamburger?

　　A. It's eighty dollars.
　　B. It's fifty-five dollars.
　　C. It's eighteen dollars.

正確答案為 A

A. **Questions 1-2**

B. **Question 3**

C. <u>Questions 4-5</u>

D. <u>Question 6</u>

請翻頁 ▯▯▷

E. Question 7

F. Question 8

G. **Question 9**

H. **Question 10**

請翻頁 ▉▉▉⟹

第二部份： 問答

本部份共 10 題，每題錄音機會播出一個問句或直述句，
每題播出一次，聽後請從試題冊上 A、B、C 三個選項
中，選出一個最適合的回答或回應，並在答案紙上塗黑
作答。

例：

（聽） Good morning, Kevin. How are you?

（看）　A. I'm fine, thank you.
　　　　B. I'm in the living room.
　　　　C. My name is Kevin.

正確答案為 A

11. A. I like to paint and collect stamps.
　　B. It's a good habit to get up early.
　　C. I work in a café part-time.

12. A. I had my legs broken.
　　B. The other guy ran a red light.
　　C. It wasn't your fault.

13. A. Let's ask the ticket seller.
　　B. It was wonderful.
　　C. It's my favorite sport, too.

14. A. You don't need to wear a suit. The party is informal.
　　B. That suit fits you very well.
　　C. Yes. It's really your style.

15. A. No, I have.

    B. Yes, I didn't yet.

    C. Yes, I did.

16. A. Yes, you can park on this street.

    B. The park is across the street.

    C. Yes, it is. Where do you want to go?

17. A. I'll watch it in the morning if you watch it in the afternoon.

    B. Yes. I've been looking for it.

    C. No. I've been studying.

18. A. I always buy it in the market.

    B. My mother made pancakes today.

    C. I like to eat a sandwich for breakfast.

19. A. I'm expecting the vacation, too.

    B. Me, too. My favorite season is winter.

    C. Did you have a good time?

20. A. I see him every day.

    B. Yes, but sometimes we argue.

    C. No, we usually go out with friends.

請 翻 頁 ⃕

第三部份： 簡短對話

本部份共 10 題，每題錄音機會播出一段對話及一個相關的問題，每題播出兩次，聽後請從試題冊上 A、B、C 三個選項中，選出一個最適合的回答，並在答案紙上塗黑作答。

例：

(聽) (Woman) Good afternoon, ...Mr. Davis?

(Man) Yes. I have an appointment with Dr. Sanders at two o'clock. My son Tommy has a fever.

(Woman) Oh, that's too bad. Well, please have a seat, Mr. Davis. Dr. Sanders will be right with you.

Question: Where did this conversation take place?

(看) A. In a post office.
B. In a restaurant.
C. In a doctor's office.

正確答案為 C

21. A. His brother gave it to him.
B. He borrowed some money from the bank.
C. He took all his money out of the bank.

22. A. They will see each other often.
B. They will have all of their classes together.
C. They should join the same art class.

23. A. He must pay a total of
       $300.
    B. He kept the movie
       for six days.
    C. He must pay for a total
       of four days' rental.

24. A. The steak or chicken.
    B. Salad, dessert and
       coffee.
    C. He'll have the steak.

25. A. His car was stolen.
    B. He was sentenced to 5
       years in prison.
    C. He had to give the
       woman a new car.

26. A. Because he likes the
       DJ.
    B. Because his teacher
       told him to.
    C. Because he likes
       English music.

27. A. Sogo does not sell
       Nike sports shoes.
    B. Sogo might have some
       shoes on sale.
    C. Sogo is the cheapest
       place to buy the new
       Nikes.

28. A. On Monday.
    B. In two days.
    C. It will be an English
       test.

29. A. Call the doctor
       tomorrow.
    B. Take one pill every
       four hours.
    C. She will give Johnny
       six pills.

30. A. He will go shopping
       for a new ring.
    B. He will decide to go
       to the movie.
    C. He does not know.

請 翻 頁 ◖⟹

初級英語聽力檢定⑦詳解

第一部份

For questions number 1 and 2, please look at picture A.

1. (**A**) What are they doing?

　　A. They are waving goodbye to each other.

　　B. They are shaking hands.

　　C. They are crying.

　　* wave〔wev〕v. 揮手表示

　　　wave goodbye to sb. 向某人揮手告別

　　　each other 彼此　　***shake hands*** 握手

　　　cry〔kraɪ〕v. 哭

2. (**C**) Please look at picture A again. What will the woman
　　　with the baggage probably do next?

　　A. She'll return to her house.

　　B. She'll get out of the car.

　　C. She'll take a plane.

　　* baggage〔'bægɪdʒ〕n. 行李

　　　probably〔'prɑbəblɪ〕adv. 大概；或許

　　　next〔nɛkst〕adv. 接下來；然後

　　　return〔rɪ'tɝn〕v. 返回　　***get out of*** 自～下車

　　　take〔tek〕v. 搭乘　　plane〔plen〕n. 飛機

For question number 3, please look at picture B.

3. (**B**) What are the people in front of the stage doing?

    A. They are actors.

    B. They are watching the show.

    C. They are dancing.

    * *in front of* 在…的前面   stage〔sted3〕*n.* 舞台

    actor〔'æktə〕*n.* 演員   show〔ʃo〕*n.* 表演

    dance〔dæns〕*v.* 跳舞

For questions number 4 and 5, please look at picture C.

4. (**B**) What is the boy doing?

    A. He's washing his hands.

    B. He's helping his mother with the dishes.

    C. He's having dinner.

    * wash〔waʃ〕*v.* 洗   *help sb. with sth.* 幫助某人某事

    dishes〔'dɪʃɪz〕*n. pl.* 碗盤   have〔hæv〕*v.* 吃；喝

5. (**B**) Please look at picture C again. Where are they
washing?

    A. At the dining table.

    B. At the sink.

    C. At the dishwasher.

    * *dining table* 餐桌

    sink〔sɪŋk〕*n.* (廚房的)流理臺；水槽

    dishwasher〔'dɪʃ,waʃə〕*n.* 洗碗機

For question number 6, please look at picture D.

6. (**C**) What is on the table?

　　　　A. She is talking on her cell phone.

　　　　B. She is putting on makeup.

　　　　C. There is a mirror.

　　　* ***cell phone*** 手機　　makeup〔'mek,ʌp〕*n.* 化妝；化妝品

　　　　put on makeup 化妝　　mirror〔'mɪrɚ〕*n.* 鏡子

For question number 7, please look at picture E.

7. (**A**) What is in the mailman's hand?

　　　　A. It is a letter.

　　　　B. It is a hat.

　　　　C. It is behind the fence.

　　　* mailman〔'mel,mæn〕*n.* 郵差

　　　　letter〔'lɛtɚ〕*n.* 信　　hat〔hæt〕*n.* 帽子

　　　　behind〔bɪ'haɪnd〕*prep.* 在…的後面

　　　　fence〔fɛns〕*n.* 柵欄；籬笆

For question number 8, please look at picture F.

8. (**B**) Who is posing for the picture?

　　　　A. A photographer.

　　　　B. Three tourists.

　　　　C. They are posed in front of the trees.

　　　* pose〔poz〕*v.* (使) 擺姿勢　　picture〔'pɪktʃɚ〕*n.* 照片

　　　　photographer〔fə'tɑgrəfɚ〕*n.* 攝影師

　　　　tourist〔'tʊrɪst〕*n.* 遊客

For question number 9, please look at picture G.

9. (**C**) What do they play in the afternoon?

　　A. They play at three o'clock.

　　B. They play in the living room.

　　C. They play piano and guitar.

　　* *living room* 客廳　　piano〔ˋpɪæno〕*n.* 鋼琴

　　guitar〔gɪˋtɑr〕*n.* 吉他

For question number 10, please look at picture H.

10. (**C**) How will he fix the car?

　　A. He is a mechanic.

　　B. It is out of order.

　　C. With some tools.

　　* fix〔fɪks〕*v.* 修理　　mechanic〔məˋkænɪk〕*n.* 技工

　　out of order 故障　　tool〔tul〕*n.* 工具

第二部份

11. (**A**) Do you have any hobbies?

　　A. I like to paint and collect stamps.

　　B. It's a good habit to get up early.

　　C. I work in a café part-time.

　　* hobby〔ˋhɑbɪ〕*n.* 嗜好　　paint〔pent〕*v.* 繪畫

　　collect〔kəˋlɛkt〕*v.* 收集　　stamp〔stæmp〕*n.* 郵票

　　habit〔ˋhæbɪt〕*n.* 習慣　　*get up* 起床

　　café〔kəˋfe〕*n.* 咖啡廳

　　part-time〔ˋpɑrtˋtaɪm〕*adv.* 部份時間地；兼職地

12. (**B**) I heard you had a car accident. What happened?

    A. I had my legs broken.

    B. The other guy ran a red light.

    C. It wasn't your fault.

    * hear〔hɪr〕v. 聽說　　accident〔'æksədənt〕n. 車禍

    happen〔'hæpən〕v. 發生　　leg〔lɛg〕n. 腿

    break〔brek〕v. 折斷（三態變化爲：break-broke-broken）

    guy〔gaɪ〕n. 傢伙；人　　***run a red light*** 闖紅燈

    fault〔fɔlt〕n. 錯誤

13. (**A**) I wonder what time the game starts.

    A. Let's ask the ticket seller.

    B. It was wonderful.

    C. It's my favorite sport, too.

    * wonder〔'wʌndə〕v. 想知道

    game〔gem〕n. 比賽　　start〔start〕v. 開始

    ticket〔'tɪkɪt〕n. 入場券　　***ticket seller*** 售票員

    wonderful〔'wʌndəfəl〕adj. 很棒的

    favorite〔'fevərɪt〕adj. 最喜愛的　　sport〔sport〕n. 運動

14. (**C**) Do you think this dress suits me?

    A. You don't need to wear a suit. The party is informal.

    B. That suit fits you very well.

    C. Yes. It's really your style.

    * dress〔drɛs〕n. 洋裝　　suit〔sut〕v. 適合　n. 西裝；套裝

    wear〔wɛr〕v. 穿　　party〔'partɪ〕n. 派對；宴會

    informal〔ɪn'fɔrml〕adj. 非正式的

    fit〔fɪt〕v.（衣服）合身　　style〔staɪl〕n. 風格

15. (**C**) You didn't have lunch yet, did you?

    A. No, I have.   B. Yes, I didn't yet.

    C. Yes, I did.

    * yet〔jɛt〕*adv.* 還（沒）

    A. B. 須改為 No, I didn't (yet). 才能選。

16. (**C**) Is this Park Street?

    A. Yes, you can park on this street.

    B. The park is across the street.

    C. Yes, it is. Where do you want to go?

    * park〔pɑrk〕*n.* 公園 *v.* 停車

    across〔ə'krɔs〕*prep.* 在…的另一邊

17. (**C**) Have you been watching TV all morning?

    A. I'll watch it in the morning if you watch it in the afternoon.

    B. Yes. I've been looking for it.

    C. No. I've been studying.

    * ***look for*** 尋找   study〔'stʌdɪ〕*v.* 唸書

18. (**A**) Who usually makes your breakfast?

    A. I always buy it in the market.

    B. My mother made pancakes today.

    C. I like to eat a sandwich for breakfast.

    * usually〔'juʒʊəlɪ〕*adv.* 通常   make〔mek〕*v.* 做

    market〔'mɑrkɪt〕*n.* 市場   pancake〔'pæn,kek〕*n.* 鬆餅

    sandwich〔'sændwɪtʃ〕*n.* 三明治

19. (**A**) I'm really looking forward to the summer vacation.

     A. I'm expecting the vacation, too.

     B. Me, too. My favorite season is winter.

     C. Did you have a good time?

     * ***look forward to*** 期待 (= expect〔ɪkˈspɛkt〕)
     summer vacation 暑假   ***have a good time*** 玩得高興

20. (**B**) Do you and your brother usually get along?

     A. I see him every day.

     B. Yes, but sometimes we argue.

     C. No, we usually go out with friends.

     * ***get along*** 和睦相處
     sometimes〔ˈsʌm͵taɪmz〕*adv.* 有時候
     argue〔ˈɑrgjʊ〕*v.* 爭吵   ***go out*** 外出

第三部份

21. (**B**) M: I heard Tim just got a new car.

     W: Really? How did he pay for it?

     M: He borrowed some money from his brother and
        got a loan from the bank.

     Question : How did Tim get a new car?

     A. His brother gave it to him.

     B. He borrowed some money from the bank.

     C. He took all his money out of the bank.

     * get〔gɛt〕*v.* 買 (= *buy*)   ***pay for*** 付錢買～
     borrow〔ˈbɑro〕*v.* 借 (入)   loan〔lon〕*n.* 貸款
     bank〔bæŋk〕*n.* 銀行   ***out of*** 從… (= *from*)

22. (**A**)　M: Have you gotten your class schedule yet?

W: Yeah.　I've got English and math on Monday,
Wednesday and Friday.

M: Me, too.　And I've got science on Tuesday and
Thursday and art on Friday.

W: We're in the same science class, but I've got art on
Tuesday.

M: Well, I guess we'll be seeing a lot of each other.

Question : What does the man mean?

A. They will see each other often.

B. They will have all of their classes together.

C. They should join the same art class.

* schedule〔'skɛdʒul〕*n.* 時間表
  class schedule 課程表
  yeah〔jɛ〕*adv.* 是 (= *yes*)　　*have got* 有
  math〔mæθ〕*n.* 數學　science〔'saɪəns〕*n.* 自然科學
  art〔ɑrt〕*n.* 美術　*the same* 相同的
  guess〔gɛs〕*v.* 猜想
  see a lot of each other 常看見彼此
  join〔dʒɔɪn〕*v.* 參加

23. (**B**) M : Here is the movie I rented last week.

W : Okay. That will be $300.

M : What? I thought the rental fee was $100.

W : It is, but you can only keep the movie for two days. The late fee is $50 per day and you are four days late. So that's an extra $200.

Question : How many days did the man keep the movie in total?

A. He must pay a total of $300.

B. He kept the movie for six days.

C. He must pay for a total of four days' rental.

* rent〔rɛnt〕v. 租
  okay〔'oˈke〕interj. 好；沒問題（= O.K.）
  rental〔'rɛntl̩〕adj. 出租的　n. 租金
  fee〔fi〕n. 費用　　keep〔kip〕v. 持有
  late〔let〕adj. 遲的　　*late fee* 逾期費
  per〔pɚ〕prep. 每　　extra〔'ɛkstrə〕adj. 額外的
  total〔'totl̩〕n. 總數；合計
  in total 總共；合計　　pay〔pe〕v. 支付；付（錢）

24. (**A**) W : Waiter, what's good here?

M : The steak is very good and so is the chicken.

W : What comes with that?

M : A salad or soup, dessert and coffee.

W : All right. I'll have the steak, with a salad.

Question : What does the waiter recommend?

A. The steak or chicken.

B. Salad, dessert and coffee.　　C. He'll have the steak.

* waiter〔'wetɚ〕n. 服務生　　steak〔stek〕n. 牛排
  chicken〔'tʃɪkən〕n. 雞肉
  What comes with that? 附餐是什麼？
  salad〔'sæləd〕n. 沙拉　　soup〔sup〕n. 湯
  dessert〔dɪ'zɝt〕n. 餐後甜點　　coffee〔'kɔfɪ〕n. 咖啡
  All right. 好。　　recommend〔,rɛkə'mɛnd〕v. 推薦

25. (**B**)　M: Did the police ever catch the man who stole your car?

W: Yes, they did. In fact, the trial was last week.

M: What happened?

W: He was found guilty and has to spend 5 years in jail.

Question : What happened to the thief?

A. His car was stolen.

B. He was sentenced to 5 years in prison.

C. He had to give the woman a new car.

* **the police** 警方；警察
  ever〔'ɛvɚ〕adv. 至今　　catch〔kætʃ〕v. 抓到
  steal〔stil〕v. 偷（三態變化為：steal-stole-stolen）
  in fact 事實上　　trial〔'traɪəl〕n. 審判
  find〔faɪnd〕v. 裁決；判定　　guilty〔'gɪltɪ〕adj. 有罪的
  spend〔spɛnd〕v. 度過（時間）
  jail〔dʒel〕n. 監獄（= prison〔'prɪzn̩〕）
  in jail 在獄中；服刑（= **in prison**）
  sth. **happen to** sb. 某人發生某事
  thief〔θif〕n. 小偷　　sentence〔'sɛntəns〕v. 宣判

26. (**C**) W : My teacher said I should listen to English radio.
　　　　　　　　Do you ever listen to English radio programs?

　　　　　　M : I listen to an English station, but I can't understand
　　　　　　　　the DJ.

　　　　　　W : Then why do you listen to it?

　　　　　　M : I like the music.

　　　　　　Question : Why does the man like to listen to English
　　　　　　　　　　　radio programs?

　　　　　　A. Because he likes the DJ.

　　　　　　B. Because his teacher told him to.

　　　　　　C. Because he likes English music.

　　　　* ***listen to*** 聽　　　radio〔'redɪ,o〕*n.* 廣播
　　　　　ever〔'ɛvɚ〕*adv.* 曾經
　　　　　program〔'progræm〕*n.* 節目
　　　　　station〔'steʃən〕*n.* 電台
　　　　　understand〔,ʌndɚ'stænd〕*v.* 明白（某人說的話）
　　　　　DJ （廣播電台的）唱片音樂節目主持人（= *disk jockey* ）
　　　　　then〔ðɛn〕*adv.* 那麼；既然這樣

27. (**B**) W : I need some new basketball shoes.

　　　　　　M : Why don't you go to Sogo? They're having
　　　　　　　　a sale.

　　　　　　W : Do you think they'll have the new Nikes?

　　　　　　M : Probably, but those might not be on sale.

Question : What does the man say about Sogo?

A. Sogo does not sell Nike sports shoes.

B. Sogo might have some shoes on sale.

C. Sogo is the cheapest place to buy the new Nikes.

* ***basketball shoes*** 籃球鞋
Sogo〔'so'go〕*n.* 太平洋崇光百貨
Nikes〔'naɪkiz〕*n.* 耐吉 (運動鞋牌子)
sale〔sel〕*n.* 拍賣　　probably〔'prɑbəblɪ〕*adv.* 大概
on sale 拍賣中　　sports〔spɔrts〕*adj.* 運動的
sports shoes 運動鞋　　cheap〔tʃip〕*adj.* 便宜的

28. (**B**) M: Do you know when the next English test will be?

W: Yes. It will be on Wednesday.

M: Really? But it's already Monday.

W: Yeah. We don't have much time to prepare.

Question : When will the next test be held?

A. On Monday.

B. In two days.

C. It will be an English test.

* test〔tɛst〕*n.* 考試
already〔ɔl'rɛdɪ〕*adv.* 已經
prepare〔prɪ'pɛr〕*v.* 準備
hold〔hold〕*v.* 舉行
be held 舉行 (= *take place*)
in two days 再過兩天

29. (**A**) M：How long has Johnny had a fever?

W：Since last night.

M：I don't think it is too serious. Take this medicine and give him one pill every six hours. Let me know how he is tomorrow.

W：Thank you, doctor.

Question：What will Johnny's mother do?

A. Call the doctor tomorrow.

B. Take one pill every four hours.

C. She will give Johnny six pills.

* *How long~?* ~（時間）多久？　　fever〔ˈfivɚ〕*n.* 發燒
since〔sɪns〕*prep.* 自從　　serious〔ˈsɪrɪəs〕*adj.* 嚴重的
take〔tek〕*v.* 服（藥）　　medicine〔ˈmɛdəsn̩〕*n.* 藥
pill〔pɪl〕*n.* 藥丸　　*every six hours* 每隔六小時
let〔lɛt〕*v.* 讓　　call〔kɔl〕*v.* 打電話給~

30. (**C**) W：We're going to a movie tomorrow. Do you want to come?

M：I'm not sure. I might go shopping.

W：Well, give me a ring when you decide.

Question：What will the man do tomorrow?

A. He will go shopping for a new ring.

B. He will decide to go to the movie.

C. He does not know.

* *go to a movie* 去看電影　　sure〔ʃur〕*adj.* 確定的
go shopping 去購物　　ring〔rɪŋ〕*n.* 打電話；戒指
give sb. a ring 打電話給某人（= *give sb. a call*）
decide〔dɪˈsaɪd〕*v.* 決定

全民英語能力分級檢定測驗

初級測驗⑧

　　本測驗分三部份，全為三選一之選擇題，每部份各 10 題，共 30 題，作答時間約 20 分鐘。

第一部份：看圖辨義

　　本部份共 10 題，試題冊上每題有一個圖片，請聽錄音機播出一個相關的問題，與 A、B、C 三個英語敘述後，選一個與所看到圖片最相符的答案，並在答案紙上相對的圓圈內塗黑作答。每題播出一遍，問題及選項均不印在試題冊上。

例：（看）

NT$80　NT$50

（聽）

Look at the picture.　How much is the hamburger?

A. It's eighty dollars.
B. It's fifty-five dollars.
C. It's eighteen dollars.

正確答案為 A

A. <u>Questions 1-2</u>

B. <u>Question 3</u>

Mrs. Lin   Mary

C. Questions 4-5

Tim

D. Question 6

請 翻 頁 ➡

E. **Question 7**

F. **Question 8**

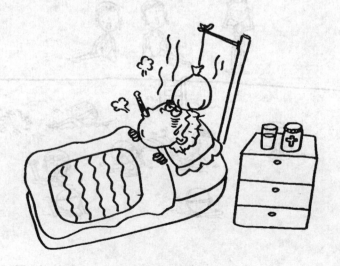

G. **Question 9**

H. **Question 10**

請翻頁

第二部份： 問答

本部份共 10 題，每題錄音機會播出一個問句或直述句，每題播出一次，聽後請從試題冊上 A、B、C 三個選項中，選出一個最適合的回答或回應，並在答案紙上塗黑作答。

例：

（聽） Good morning, Kevin. How are you?

（看） A. I'm fine, thank you.
B. I'm in the living room.
C. My name is Kevin.

正確答案為 A

11. A. Yes, I did.
B. No, thank you.
C. Same to you.

12. A. What kind?
B. Here you are.
C. We ran out.

13. A. Here you are.
B. I'll have the chicken.
C. That sounds great.

14. A. You may borrow it any time.
B. How much is it?
C. I will.

15. A. She used to live in
    Tainan.
    B. She came from the
    library.
    C. She's in my class.

16. A. I usually jog every
    morning.
    B. I usually jog five
    miles.
    C. I usually jog for
    about a half hour.

17. A. No, not yet.
    B. Yes, she hasn't.
    C. Yes, she is.

18. A. This music is all right,
    but I prefer classical
    music.
    B. Yes, I like to listen to
    music.
    C. Not really. Could you
    turn it up?

19. A. I just won the lottery!
    B. I stayed up studying
    last night.
    C. I just had my hair done.

20. A. I'll take two coffees,
    please.
    B. With cream and sugar.
    C. I take it in the café.

請 翻 頁 ▥⟹

第三部份：簡短對話

本部份共 10 題，每題錄音機會播出一段對話及一個相關的問題，每題播出兩次，聽後請從試題冊上 A、B、C 三個選項中，選出一個最適合的回答，並在答案紙上塗黑作答。

例：

（聽）(Woman)　Good afternoon, …Mr. Davis?

　　　(Man)　　Yes. I have an appointment with Dr. Sanders at two o'clock. My son Tommy has a fever.

　　　(Woman)　Oh, that's too bad. Well, please have a seat, Mr. Davis. Dr. Sanders will be right with you.

　　　Question:　Where did this conversation take place?

（看）A. In a post office.

　　　B. In a restaurant.

　　　C. In a doctor's office.

正確答案爲 C

21. A. Mark Twain is a
    better-known writer
    than Samuel Clemens.
    B. No one has ever heard
    of Samuel Clemens.
    C. Samuel Clemens and
    Mark Twain are the
    same person.

22. A. To the science lab.
    B. It's just down the hall.
    C. We don't know.

23. A. Many people are
    going around.
    B. Anna should calm
    down.
    C. It is easy to catch a
    cold now.

24. A. She cannot find the
    bus to Taipei.
    B. She cannot go to
    Taipei today.
    C. She just missed the
    bus to Taipei.

25. A. The man should
    demand a refund.
    B. The man should get
    more money from
    the bank.
    C. The man should not
    have given his money
    for the walkman.

請 翻 頁 ⫸

26. A. The students at the man's school like basketball more than the students at the woman's school do.
    B. Volleyball is the second most popular sport at the man's school.
    C. Basketball is the most popular sport at both schools.

27. A. The most popular watch.
    B. A gift.
    C. The watch in the back.

28. A. Help the man with his history homework.
    B. Ask a question about page 245.
    C. Read two more pages in the history book.

29. A. He was finishing his homework.
    B. He did it after the program.
    C. He was watching a TV program.

30. A. Put the jacket in the closet.
    B. Stop lying around.
    C. Find his jacket.

初級英語聽力檢定⑧詳解

第一部份

For questions number 1 and 2, please look at picture A.

1. (**B**) What are the two women holding?
   A. Movie tickets.
   B. Boarding passes.
   C. Handbags.

   * hold〔hold〕v. 握著；拿著　　ticket〔'tɪkɪt〕n. 入場券
     boarding〔'bordɪŋ〕n. 登機
     pass〔pæs〕n. 通行證　　***boarding pass*** 登機證
     handbag〔'hænd,bæg〕n. 手提包

2. (**C**) Please look at picture A again. What is true about the
   flight attendant?
   A. The flight attendant takes an aisle seat.
   B. The flight attendant is a male.
   C. The flight attendant is a female.

   * true〔tru〕*adj.* 眞實的；正確的
     attendant〔ə'tɛndənt〕n. 服務員
     flight attendant 空服員
     take〔tek〕v. 就（座）；佔（位置）
     aisle〔aɪl〕n.（飛機坐椅間的）走道
     seat〔sit〕n. 座位　　male〔mel〕n. 男性
     female〔'fimel〕n. 女性

For question number 3, please look at picture B.

3. (**A**) What are Mrs. Lin and Mary talking about?

　　A. Apples.

　　B. It is too expensive.

　　C. They are talking to the fruit seller.

　　* ***talk about*** 談論　　apple (ˈæpl̩) *n.* 蘋果

　　　expensive (ɪkˈspɛnsɪv) *adj.* 昂貴的

　　　seller (ˈsɛlɚ) *n.* 賣方

For questions number 4 and 5, please look at picture C.

4. (**C**) Tim must finish his breakfast by quarter to eight. How much longer can he eat?

　　A. 8:45.　　　　　　B. He can eat the egg.

　　C. Five minutes.

　　* finish (ˈfɪnɪʃ) *v.* 完成；吃完

　　　quarter (ˈkwɔrtɚ) *n.* 一刻鐘；十五分鐘

　　　by (a) quarter to eight 在七點四十五分之前

　　　egg (ɛg) *n.* 雞蛋

5. (**A**) Please look at picture C again. What does Tim eat for breakfast?

　　A. A fried egg.　　　　B. Rice soup.

　　C. Ice cream.

　　* fried (fraɪd) *adj.* 油煎的　　***fried egg*** 荷包蛋

　　　rice (raɪs) *n.* 米　　　soup (sup) *n.* 湯

　　　rice soup 稀飯　　***ice cream*** 冰淇淋

For question number 6, please look at picture D.

6. (**A**) Who is splashing in the pool?

    A. A boy.   B. Seven children.

    C. They are stretching.

* splash〔splæʃ〕v. 潑水

   pool〔pul〕n. 游泳池（= swimming pool）

   stretch〔strɛtʃ〕v. 伸展

For question number 7, please look at picture E.

7. (**B**) What is the man?

    A. He is a teacher.   B. He is a speaker.

    C. He is giving a speech.

* *What is sb.?* 某人是從事什麼工作？

   teacher〔'titʃɚ〕n. 老師   speaker〔'spikɚ〕n. 演說家

   speech〔spitʃ〕n. 演講   *give a speech* 發表演說

   lady〔'ledɪ〕n. 女士（尊稱）

   gentleman〔'dʒɛntḷmən〕n. 先生（尊稱）

   Ladies and gentlemen, … 各位女士，各位先生…（演講

    的開場白）

For question number 8, please look at picture F.

8. (**A**) What is wrong with the man?

    A. He has a fever.   B. He is in bed.

    C. He should not smoke.

* *What is wrong with sb.?* 某人怎麼了？（= *What's the*

   matter with sb.?）   fever〔'fivɚ〕n. 發燒

   in bed 躺在床上   smoke〔smok〕v. 抽煙

For question number 9, please look at picture G.

9. (**A**) What is the teacher asking?
   A. What x and y are.   B. She is teaching math.
   C. X equals five.

   * math〔mæθ〕*n.* 數學   equal〔'ikwəl〕*v.* 等於

For question number 10, please look at picture H.

10. (**B**) What does the teacher ask the children to do?
    A. Learn to play the piano.
    B. Sing a song.
    C. Sit quietly.

    * piano〔pɪ'æno〕*n.* 鋼琴   quietly〔'kwaɪətlɪ〕*adv.* 安靜地

第二部份

11. (**C**) Good luck on the exam.
    A. Yes, I did.   B. No, thank you.
    C. Same to you.

    * luck〔lʌk〕*n.* 運氣   exam〔ɪg'zæm〕*n.* 考試
    Same to you. 你也是。

12. (**A**) Can you pick up some juice for me at the Seven-Eleven?
    A. What kind?   B. Here you are.
    C. We ran out.

    * ***pick up*** 拿；買   juice〔dʒus〕*n.* 果汁
    kind〔kaɪnd〕*n.* 種類   ***Here you are.*** 你要的東西在
    這裡；拿去吧。(= *Here it is.*)   ***run out*** 跑出去

13. (**C**) May I take you to lunch?

    A. Here you are.   B. I'll have the chicken.

    C. That sounds great.

    * take〔tek〕v. 帶去   have〔hæv〕v. 吃

    chicken〔'tʃɪkən〕n. 雞肉   sound〔saʊnd〕v. 聽起來

    great〔gret〕adj. 很棒的

14. (**C**) Give me a call when you get there.

    A. You may borrow it any time.

    B. How much is it?

    C. I will.

    * *give sb. a call* 打電話給某人   *get there* 到那裡

    borrow〔'baro〕v. 借（入）

15. (**A**) Where does the new student come from?

    A. She used to live in Tainan.

    B. She came from the library.

    C. She's in my class.

    * *used to V.* 以前～   *Tainan* 台南

    library〔'laɪ,brɛrɪ〕n. 圖書館

16. (**C**) How long do you usually jog?

    A. I usually jog every morning.

    B. I usually jog five miles.

    C. I usually jog for about a half hour.

    * *How long～?* ～多久？   usually〔'juʒʊəlɪ〕adv. 通常

    jog〔dʒɑg〕v. 慢跑   mile〔maɪl〕n. 英哩

    half〔hæf〕adj. 一半的   *a half hour* 半小時

17. (**A**) Your sister hasn't been to England, has she?

    A. No, not yet.

    B. Yes, she hasn't.

    C. Yes, she is.

    * ***have been to*** 曾經去過　　England〔'ɪŋglənd〕 *n.* 英國
    yet〔jɛt〕 *adv.* 還（沒）　　B. 須改爲 No, she hasn't.
    才能選；C. 須改爲 Yes, she has. 才能選。

18. (**C**) Can you hear the music all right?

    A. This music is all right, but I prefer classical music.

    B. Yes, I like to listen to music.

    C. Not really. Could you turn it up?

    * ***all right*** 順利地；很好地　　prefer〔prɪ'fɜ〕 *v.* 比較喜歡
    classical〔'klæsɪkl̩〕 *adj.* 古典的　***listen to*** 聽
    turn up （音量）調大聲

19. (**B**) You look exhausted. Why?

    A. I just won the lottery!

    B. I stayed up studying last night.

    C. I just had my hair done.

    * look〔lʊk〕 *v.* 看起來
    exhausted〔ɪg'zɔstɪd〕 *adj.* 精疲力竭的
    win〔wɪn〕 *v.* 贏得（三態變化爲：win-won-won）
    lottery〔'latərɪ〕 *n.* 彩券；樂透　　***stay up*** 熬夜
    study〔'stʌdɪ〕 *v.* 唸書　***have*** + 受詞 + ***p.p.*** （受詞）被~
    hair〔hɛr〕 *n.* 頭髮　***have one's hair done*** 某人做頭髮

20. (**B**) How do you take your coffee?

    A. I'll take two coffees, please.

    B. With cream and sugar.   C. I take it in the café.

    * take〔tek〕*v.* 吃；喝   coffee〔'kɔfɪ〕*n.* 咖啡

    How do you take your coffee? 你的咖啡要加糖或奶精嗎？

    cream〔krim〕*n.* 奶油；奶精   sugar〔'ʃugɚ〕*n.* 糖

    café〔kə'fe〕*n.* 咖啡廳

第三部份

21. (**C**) W: Have you ever heard of Samuel Clemens?

    M: Sure. He was a very famous writer.

    W: Really? Then how come I never heard of him?

    M: Well, he's better known as Mark Twain.

    Question : What does the man mean?

    A. Mark Twain is a better-known writer than Samuel Clemens.

    B. No one has ever heard of Samuel Clemens.

    C. Samuel Clemens and Mark Twain are the same person.

    * ***hear of*** 聽說過   sure〔ʃur〕*adv.* 當然（= *of course*）

    famous〔'feməs〕*adj.* 有名的   writer〔'raɪtɚ〕*n.* 作家

    then〔ðɛn〕*adv.* 那麼   ***how come*** 為什麼（後面接直述句）

    be known as 因～（身份、名稱）而聞名

    better〔'bɛtɚ〕*adv.* 更

    Mark Twain 馬克吐溫（美國作家）

    mean〔min〕*v.* 意思是

    better-known〔'bɛtɚ'non〕*adj.* 更出名的（well-known 的

    比較級）   ever〔'ɛvɚ〕*adv.* 曾經   ***the same*** 相同的

22. (**C**) W: Excuse me, do you know where the science lab is?

M: Sure. It's just down the hall.

W: Thanks.

M: Are you a new student here?

W: Yes. Today is my first day.

Question : Where is the new student from?

A. To the science lab.

B. It's just down the hall.

C. We don't know.

* ***excuse me*** 對不起　　science〔'saɪəns〕*n.* 自然科學
lab〔læb〕*n.* 實驗室（= laboratory〔'læbrə,torɪ〕）
down〔daʊn〕*prep.* 在⋯盡頭；沿著　　hall〔hɔl〕*n.* 走廊

23. (**C**) M: I haven't seen Anna for a few days, have you?

W: No. I heard she came down with a cold.

M: Many people have. There's something going around.

Question : What does the man mean?

A. Many people are going around.

B. Anna should calm down.

C. It is easy to catch a cold now.

* hear〔hɪr〕*v.* 聽說
come down with 因～而病倒；罹患
cold〔kold〕*n.* 感冒
go around （疾病等）流行、散佈；（人）四處走走
calm down 冷靜下來　　***catch a cold*** 感冒

24. (**C**) W: Was that the bus for Taipei?

M: It sure was.

W: Do you know when the next one is?

M: Not for a half hour.

Question : What is true about the woman?

A. She cannot find the bus to Taipei.

B. She cannot go to Taipei today.

C. She just missed the bus to Taipei.

* for〔fɔr〕*prep.* 朝…方向去；往

just〔dʒʌst〕*adv.* 剛剛　　miss〔mɪs〕*v.* 錯過

25. (**A**) M: Oh, no!

W: What happened?

M: My walkman isn't working. And I just bought it yesterday.

W: You should get your money back.

Question : What does the woman mean?

A. The man should demand a refund.

B. The man should get more money from the bank.

C. The man should not have given his money for the walkman.

* happen〔'hæpən〕*v.* 發生

walkman〔'wɔkmən〕*n.* 隨身聽

work〔wɜk〕*v.* (機器等) 運轉　　*get back* 取回

demand〔dɪ'mænd〕*v.* 要求

refund〔'ri,fʌnd〕*n.* 退錢　　bank〔bæŋk〕*n.* 銀行

should not have + *p.p.* 當初不應該 (表過去不該做而做)

26.(**C**) M: What's the most popular sport at your school?

W: It's basketball, of course, but I like volleyball better.

M: I like volleyball, too, but I prefer baseball.

W: Is that the most popular sport at your school?

M: No, but it's a close second to basketball.

Question : What do we know from this conversation?

A. The students at the man's school like basketball more than the students at the woman's school do.

B. Volleyball is the second most popular sport at the man's school.

C. Basketball is the most popular sport at both schools.

* popular〔'pɑpjələ〕adj. 受歡迎的
sport〔sport〕n. 運動　　*of course* 當然
volleyball〔'vɑlɪ,bɔl〕n. 排球
baseball〔'bes,bɔl〕n. 棒球
close〔klos〕adj. 接近的;(比賽)勢均力敵的
second〔'sɛkənd〕n. 第二名
be a close second 與第一名差距很小的第二名
conversation〔,kɑnvə'seʃən〕n. 對話

27.(**B**) W: Excuse me, can I see that watch in the back?

M: Of course. It's our most popular style.

W: I'm not sure.

M: It looks very nice on you.

W: Oh, it's not for me. It's for my mother.

Question : What does the woman want to buy?

A. The most popular watch.

B. A gift.

C. The watch in the back.

* back〔bæk〕*n.* 後面　　style〔staɪl〕*n.* 款式
sure〔ʃʊr〕*adj.* 確定的
It looks very nice on you. 你戴起來很好看。
gift〔gɪft〕*n.* 禮物（= *present*）

28. (**B**) W: Have you finished reading the history chapter?

M: Not yet. I'm only on page 243.

W: Well, when you get to page 245, let me know.
There's something there I don't understand.

Question : What will the woman do?

A. Help the man with his history homework.

B. Ask a question about page 245.

C. Read two more pages in the history book.

* finish〔'fɪnɪʃ〕*v.* 完成　　history〔'hɪstrɪ〕*n.* 歷史
chapter〔'tʃæptɚ〕*n.*（書的）章
not yet 尚未；還沒　　page〔pedʒ〕*n.*（書的）頁
get to 到達　　let〔lɛt〕*v.* 讓
understand〔,ʌndɚ'stænd〕*v.* 了解
help sb. with sth. 幫助某人某事
homework〔'hom,wɝk〕*n.* 家庭作業
question〔'kwɛstʃən〕*n.* 問題

29. (**C**) W: Hey, did you finish your homework?

M: Almost, Mom. I'll do it right after this program.

W: No. Finish it before you watch TV.

Question : What was the boy doing when his mother came in?

A. He was finishing his homework.

B. He did it after the program.

C. He was watching a TV program.

* hey〔he〕*interj.* 喂（用以喚起注意等）

almost〔'ɔl,most〕*adv.* 幾乎；差不多

right〔raɪt〕*adv.* 立即；馬上

program〔'progræm〕*n.* 節目　　***come in*** 進來

30. (**A**) M: Is this your jacket?

W: Yes, it is. Why?

M: You should hang it up, not leave it lying around.

Question : What does the man want the woman to do?

A. Put the jacket in the closet.

B. Stop lying around.

C. Find his jacket.

* jacket〔'dʒækɪt〕*n.* 夾克　　***hang sth. up*** 把某物掛起來

leave〔liv〕*v.* 使（處於某種狀態）

lie〔laɪ〕*v.* （東西）平放；（人）說謊

around〔ə'raund〕*adv.* 到處　　put〔put〕*v.* 放

closet〔'klɑzɪt〕*n.* 衣櫥

全民英語能力分級檢定測驗

初級測驗⑨

　　本測驗分三部份，全為三選一之選擇題，每部份各 10 題，共 30 題，作答時間約 20 分鐘。

第一部份：看圖辨義

　　　　本部份共 10 題，試題冊上每題有一個圖片，請聽錄音機播出一個相關的問題，與 A、B、C 三個英語敘述後，選一個與所看到圖片最相符的答案，並在答案紙上相對的圓圈內塗黑作答。每題播出一遍，問題及選項均不印在試題冊上。

例：（看）

NT$80　　NT$50

（聽）

Look at the picture.　How much is the hamburger?

　　A.　It's eighty dollars.
　　B.　It's fifty-five dollars.
　　C.　It's eighteen dollars.

正確答案為 A

A. <u>Questions 1-2</u>

B. <u>Question 3</u>

C. **Questions 4-5**

D. **Question 6**

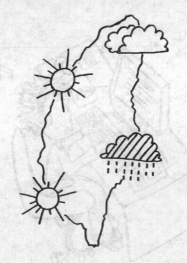

請 翻 頁 ▐ ⟹

E. **Question 7**

F. **Question 8**

G. **Question 9**

H. **Question 10**

請翻頁 ▯▯▷

第二部份：問答

　　　本部份共 10 題，每題錄音機會播出一個問句或直述句，
每題播出一次，聽後請從試題冊上 A、B、C 三個選項
中，選出一個最適合的回答或回應，並在答案紙上塗黑
作答。

例：

（聽）Good morning, Kevin.　How are you?

（看）A.　I'm fine, thank you.
　　　B.　I'm in the living room.
　　　C.　My name is Kevin.

　　　正確答案為 A

11. A. I bought it at the
　　　bookstore.
　　B. I use it to look up
　　　new words.
　　C. It's on the table.

12. A. It's on the fifth floor.
　　B. Sorry, but I'm going
　　　the other way.
　　C. You're welcome.　I
　　　hope you like it.

13. A. Yes.　Help yourself.
　　B. I often read books,
　　　too.
　　C. Sorry.　I don't know
　　　how to operate it.

14. A. Sorry.　I don't have
　　　a watch.
　　B. It is 2:00 now.
　　C. At 12:30.

15. A. It's not broken.
    B. I'll have the daily special.
    C. No, thanks. I'm not hungry.

16. A. Yes. I heard from him yesterday.
    B. No, I didn't.
    C. Of course.

17. A. Oh, I wish I could.
    B. No, I didn't go.
    C. I would like tomorrow.

18. A. That's terrible. Was anyone hurt?
    B. What time did the train leave?
    C. How is he doing?

19. A. I'll give you a hand.
    B. No problem.
    C. You're too kind.

20. A. I had to study for a big exam.
    B. I will go hiking on Saturday.
    C. It's our last chance to have fun before the exam.

請翻頁 ⟹

第三部份： 簡短對話

本部份共 10 題，每題錄音機會播出一段對話及一個相關的問題，每題播出兩次，聽後請從試題冊上 A、B、C 三個選項中，選出一個最適合的回答，並在答案紙上塗黑作答。

例：

（聽）(Woman)　Good afternoon, …Mr. Davis?

　　　(Man)　　Yes.　I have an appointment with Dr. Sanders at two o'clock.　My son Tommy has a fever.

　　　(Woman)　Oh, that's too bad.　Well, please have a seat, Mr. Davis.　Dr. Sanders will be right with you.

　　　Question:　Where did this conversation take place?

（看）A.　In a post office.

　　　B.　In a restaurant.

　　　C.　In a doctor's office.

正確答案爲 C

21. A. It is his turn.
　　B. He forgot to do it last week.
　　C. His sister promised to do it next week.

22. A. The Music Club.
　　B. The Movie Club.
　　C. She decided not to join a club at last.

23. A. He will eat his food
      without pepper.
    B. He will go out to buy
      some pepper.
    C. He cannot find the pepper.

24. A. He wants to read the
      newspaper.
    B. He wants to see a movie.
    C. He wants the woman
      to show him where
      the movie theater is.

25. A. Boiled tea with milk.
    B. Eggs, bacon, and tea.
    C. Black tea with boiled milk.

26. A. A pair of shoes.
    B. A registration fee.
    C. With cash.

27. A. The mechanic should buy
      him a new car.
    B. Repairing the car cost as
      much as buying a new one.
    C. He does not want the old
      car anymore.

28. A. It's all right that she
      missed the test.
    B. He is happy that
      she is all right now.
    C. She will have to
      take the test later
      today.

29. A. There was a traffic
      accident on the road
      ahead.
    B. They were in a
      terrible accident.
    C. They did not leave
      their house on time.

30. A. The man's jacket
      was a birthday
      present.
    B. The woman will
      give the man a coat
      for his birthday.
    C. The woman
      received a coat on
      her last birthday.

請 翻 頁 ▌▶

初級英語聽力檢定⑨詳解

第一部份

For questions number 1 and 2, please look at picture A.

1. (**B**) What is in the girl's left hand?

    A. An ice cream.

    B. A doll.

    C. A dog.

    * left〔lɛft〕*adj.* 左邊的

      ice cream 冰淇淋

      doll〔dɑl〕*n.* 洋娃娃；玩偶

2. (**A**) Please look at picture A again. What happened to her ice cream?

    A. It has melted.

    B. It has been eaten up by the dog.

    C. It was not her favorite flavor.

    * *happen to* 發生於

      melt〔mɛlt〕*v.* 融化

      eat up 吃完

      favorite〔'fevərɪt〕*adj.* 最喜愛的

      flavor〔'flevə〕*n.* 味道；口味

For question number 3, please look at picture B.

3. (**B**) How does the officer do his work?

    A. He directs traffic.

    B. He blows a whistle.

    C. His work is very difficult.

    * officer〔'ɔfəsə〕n. 警察 (= *police officer*)
      direct〔də'rɛkt〕v. 指揮   traffic〔'træfɪk〕n. 交通
      blow〔blo〕v. 吹響   whistle〔'hwɪsḷ〕n. 哨子
      difficult〔'dɪfə,kʌlt〕adj. 困難的

For questions number 4 and 5, please look at picture C.

4. (**C**) What is the woman using?

    A. The paper.

    B. A photocopy.

    C. A copy machine.

    * use〔juz〕v. 使用   paper〔'pepə〕n. 紙
      photocopy〔'fotə,kɑpɪ〕n. 影本
      machine〔mə'ʃin〕n. 機器   *copy machine* 影印機

5. (**B**) Please look at picture C again. Lunch time is 12:20.
    How long does the woman need to wait?

    A. One hour.

    B. Eighty minutes.

    C. Half an hour.

    * need〔nid〕v. 需要   wait〔wet〕v. 等待
      How long~? ～多久？   hour〔aʊr〕n. 小時
      minute〔'mɪnɪt〕n. 分鐘   half〔hæf〕adj. 一半的
      half an hour 半小時

For question number 6, please look at picture D.

6. (**B**) What is the weather like in southwest Taiwan?

  A. It is raining.

  B. It is clear.

  C. It is cloudy.

  * weather〔'wɛðɚ〕*n.* 天氣

   southwest〔,saʊθ'wɛst〕*adj.* 西南部的

   rain〔ren〕*v.* 下雨

   clear〔klɪr〕*adj.*（天空）無雲的；晴朗的

   cloudy〔'klaʊdɪ〕*adj.* 多雲的；陰天的

For question number 7, please look at picture E.

7. (**A**) What will the man do to celebrate?

  A. Light the firecrackers.

  B. He is celebrating New Year.

  C. He is very happy.

  * celebrate〔'sɛlə,bret〕*v.* 慶祝　　light〔laɪt〕*v.* 點燃

   firecracker〔'faɪr,krækɚ〕*n.* 鞭炮　　***New Year*** 新年

For question number 8, please look at picture F.

8. (**C**) What is the student doing?

  A. He likes to play computer games.

  B. He is in the chair.

  C. He is listening to music.

  * ***computer games*** 電玩遊戲　　***listen to*** 聽

   music〔'mjuzɪk〕*n.* 音樂

For question number 9, please look at picture G.

9. (**A**) Who is on the board?

    A. A boy.

    B. He is windsurfing.

    C. A lake.

    * board〔bord〕*n.*（木）板

    windsurf〔'wɪnd,sɜf〕*v.* 作風帆衝浪運動

    lake〔lek〕*n.* 湖

For question number 10, please look at picture H.

10. (**B**) How do they play with the tennis ball?

    A. Tennis is very good exercise.

    B. They hit it with rackets.

    C. It is very tiring.

    * ***play with*** 玩   tennis〔'tɛnɪs〕*n.* 網球

    exercise〔'ɛksɚ,saɪz〕*n.* 運動   hit〔hɪt〕*v.* 打

    racket〔'rækɪt〕*n.* 球拍   tiring〔'taɪrɪŋ〕*adj.* 累人的

第二部份

11. (**C**) Do you have the dictionary?

    A. I bought it at the bookstore.

    B. I use it to look up new words.

    C. It's on the table.

    * dictionary〔'dɪkʃən,ɛrɪ〕*n.* 字典

    bookstore〔'buk,stor〕*n.* 書店

    look up 查閱

12. (**B**) Can you give me a lift to the record store?

     A. It's on the fifth floor.

     B. Sorry, but I'm going the other way.

     C. You're welcome. I hope you like it.

    * lift〔lɪft〕*n.* 順便搭載　　***give sb. a lift*** 順便搭載某人
      record〔ˈrɛkəd〕*n.* 唱片
      record store 唱片行（= *music store*）
      floor〔flor〕*n.* 樓層　　***go the other way*** 走另一邊
      You're welcome. 不客氣。

13. (**A**) Is this your magazine?

     A. Yes. Help yourself.   B. I often read books, too.

     C. Sorry. I don't know how to operate it.

    * magazine〔ˌmægəˈzin〕*n.* 雜誌　　***Help yourself.*** 自己拿。
      operate〔ˈɑpəˌret〕*v.* 操作

14. (**C**) Can you tell me when the next show is?

     A. Sorry. I don't have a watch.

     B. It is 2:00 now.   C. At 12:30.

    * show〔ʃo〕*n.* 表演；電影放映

15. (**C**) Can I fix you something to eat?

     A. It's not broken.   B. I'll have the daily special.

     C. No, thanks. I'm not hungry.

    * fix〔fɪks〕*v.* 準備（食物）　　***Can I fix you something***
      to eat? 你要我弄什麼東西給你吃嗎？
      broken〔ˈbrokən〕*adj.* 損壞的　　daily〔ˈdelɪ〕*adj.* 每日的
      special〔ˈspɛʃəl〕*n.* 特餐　　hungry〔ˈhʌŋgrɪ〕*adj.* 飢餓的

16. (**C**) Have you ever heard of Thomas Edison?

    A. Yes. I heard from him yesterday.

    B. No, I didn't.   C. Of course.

    * ever ('ɛvɚ) adv. 曾經   *hear of* 聽說過

    Thomas Edison 愛迪生（美國發明家）

    hear from sb. 得到某人的消息；收到某人的來信

    Of course. 當然。

17. (**A**) Would you like to go to the beach with us tomorrow?

    A. Oh, I wish I could.   B. No, I didn't go.

    C. I would like tomorrow.

    * *would like to V.* 想要～   beach (bitʃ) n. 海灘

    wish (wɪʃ) v. 希望；但願

18. (**C**) I ran into Jim at the station yesterday.

    A. That's terrible. Was anyone hurt?

    B. What time did the train leave?

    C. How is he doing?

    * *run into* 偶遇；撞到   station ('steʃən) n. 車站

    terrible ('tɛrəbḷ) adj. 可怕的

    hurt (hɝt) v. 使受傷（三態同形）   leave (liv) v. 離開

    How is sb. doing? 某人過得如何？

19. (**B**) Hand me that book, will you?

    A. I'll give you a hand.   B. No problem.

    C. You're too kind.

    * hand (hænd) v. 拿給   *give sb. a hand* 幫助某人

    No problem. 沒問題。   kind (kaɪnd) adj. 好心的

20. (**A**)　What did you do last weekend?

A.　I had to study for a big exam.

B.　I will go hiking on Saturday.

C.　It's our last chance to have fun before the exam.

* last〔 læst 〕*adj.* 上個的；最後的
weekend〔'wik'ɛnd〕*n.* 週末　　***have to V.*** 必須～
study〔'stʌdɪ〕*v.* 唸書　　big〔 bɪg 〕*adj.* 重要的
exam〔 ɪg'zæm 〕*n.* 考試　　***go hiking*** 去健行；去爬山
chance〔 tʃæns 〕*n.* 機會　　***have fun*** 玩得愉快

第三部份

21. (**C**)　M：Did you take out the garbage?　It's your turn, you
　　　　　　know.

W：Oh, I forgot.　And I'm really busy.

M：I suppose you want me to do it for you.

W：Could you?　I'll do it for you all next week.

M：Oh, all right.

Question：Why will the man take out the garbage?

A.　It is his turn.

B.　He forgot to do it last week.

C.　His sister promised to do it next week.

* ***take out*** 拿出去　　garbage〔'gɑrbɪdʒ〕*n.* 垃圾
turn〔 tɝn 〕*n.* 輪流　　***it's one's turn*** 輪到某人
forget〔 fɚ'gɛt 〕*v.* 忘記　　suppose〔 sə'poz 〕*v.* 猜想
all right 好　　promise〔'prɑmɪs〕*v.* 答應

22. (**B**) M: Have you chosen a school club yet?

W: No. I cannot decide between the Music Club and the Movie Club.

M: They both sound like fun. I chose the latter.

W: Then I'll join that one, too.

Question : Which club will the woman join?

A. The Music Club.　　B. The Movie Club.

C. She decided not to join a club at last.

* choose〔tʃuz〕v. 選擇（三態變化為：choose-chose-chosen）
club〔klʌb〕n. 俱樂部；社團　　*school club* 社團
decide〔dɪ'saɪd〕v. 決定
between〔bə'twin〕*prep.* 在…之間
sound〔saʊnd〕v. 聽起來
sound like fun 聽起來很有趣　　*the latter* 後者
join〔dʒɔɪn〕v. 參加　　*at last* 最後

23. (**A**) M: Would you pass the pepper, please?

W: Oh, sorry. We're all out of pepper.

M: That's all right. I can do without.

Question : What does the man mean?

A. He will eat his food without pepper.

B. He will go out to buy some pepper.

C. He cannot find the pepper.

* pass〔pæs〕v. 傳遞　　pepper〔'pɛpɚ〕n. 胡椒粉
be out of 用光　　*can do without* 沒有…也行
mean〔min〕v. 意思是　　*go out* 外出

24. (**B**) M: Have you seen today's paper?

W: No. Why?

M: I want to look at the movie section and see what time the show starts.

Question : What does the man want to do today?

A. He wants to read the newspaper.

B. He wants to see a movie.

C. He wants the woman to show him where the movie theater is.

* paper〔'pepɚ〕*n.* 報紙（= *newspaper*）
  look at 看　　section〔'sɛkʃən〕*n.*（報紙的）欄
  show〔ʃo〕*n.* 電影放映　*v.* 對著（某人）指出（路）
  start〔stɑrt〕*v.* 開始　***see a movie*** 看電影
  movie theater 電影院

25. (**B**) W: May I take your order?

M: Yes. I'll have eggs and bacon, please.

W: How would you like your eggs?

M: Boiled. Oh, and I'll have black tea with milk on the side.

Question : What does the man want for breakfast?

A. Boiled tea with milk.　　B. Eggs, bacon, and tea.

C. Black tea with boiled milk.

* ***May I take your order?*** 可以幫你點餐了嗎？
  have〔hæv〕*v.* 吃　　egg〔ɛg〕*n.* 雞蛋
  bacon〔'bekən〕*n.* 培根
  How would you like your eggs? 你希望雞蛋如何烹調？
  boiled〔bɔɪld〕*adj.* 煮熟的；煮沸的　***black tea*** 紅茶
  milk〔mɪlk〕*n.* 牛奶　　***on the side*** 另外

26. (**A**) M: Excuse me, where can I pay for these?

W: You can take those to the cash register in the shoe department.

M: Can't I pay here?

W: I'm sorry you have to pay for the items in the department where they are sold.

Question : What does the man want to pay for?

A. A pair of shoes.　　　B. A registration fee.

C. With cash.

* *excuse me* 對不起　*pay for* 付錢買~

cash〔kæʃ〕 n. 現金　register〔'rɛdʒɪstɚ〕 n. 收銀機

cash register 收銀機　shoe〔ʃu〕 n. 鞋子

department〔dɪ'partmənt〕 n. 部門

pay〔pe〕 v. 付錢　sorry〔'sɔrɪ〕 adj. 抱歉的；遺憾的

item〔'aɪtəm〕 n. 項目；物品　*a pair of* 一雙

registration〔,rɛdʒɪ'streʃən〕 n. 登記；註冊；掛號

fee〔fi〕 n. 費用

27. (**B**) W: Well, the car is ready.　Here is the bill for the repairs.

M: What?　I didn't know it would be this expensive.

W: Well, it was pretty badly damaged.

M: If I'd known it would cost this much, I would have just bought a new car!

Question : What does the man mean?

A. The mechanic should buy him a new car.

B. Repairing the car cost as much as buying a new one.

C. He does not want the old car anymore.

* ready (ˈrɛdɪ) adj. 準備好的   bill (bɪl) n. 帳單
repairs (rɪˈpɛrz) n. pl. 修理工作   this (ðɪs) adv. 這麼
expensive (ɪkˈspɛnsɪv) adj. 昂貴的
pretty (ˈprɪtɪ) adv. 相當   badly (ˈbædlɪ) adv. 嚴重地
damage (ˈdæmɪdʒ) v. 毀壞   cost (kɔst) v. 花費
mechanic (məˈkænɪk) n. 技工   repair (rɪˈpɛr) v. 修理
as much as 跟…一樣多   ***not…anymore*** 不再

28. (**C**) W: I'm sorry I didn't come to class today.

M: What happened?

W: I was sick and my mother took me to the doctor this morning.

M: Well, that's all right then. But you missed an important test. You can make it up this afternoon.

Question : What does the teacher tell the woman?

A. It's all right that she missed the test.

B. He is happy that she is all right now.

C. She will have to take the test later today.

* sick (sɪk) adj. 生病的   take (tek) v. 帶去
that's all right 沒關係
then (ðɛn) adv. 那麼；既然這樣   miss (mɪs) v. 錯過
important (ɪmˈpɔrtn̩t) adj. 重要的
test (tɛst) n. 考試   ***make up*** 補考
all right 沒問題的；(健康) 良好的
later (ˈletɚ) adv. 較晚地

29. (**A**) W : This traffic is terrible! We're going to be late!

M : It's always bad at rush hour.

W : Yeah, but this is even worse than usual.

M : Maybe there was an accident.

W : You're right. There it is ahead.

Question : Why are the speakers stuck in traffic?

A. There was a traffic accident on the road ahead.

B. They were in a terrible accident.

C. They did not leave their house on time.

* traffic〔'træfɪk〕*n.* 交通

terrible〔'tɛrəbl̩〕*adj.* 糟糕的

late〔let〕*adj.* 遲到的   ***rush hour*** 交通尖峰時間

yeah〔jɛ〕*adv.* 是的 (= *yes*)

even〔'ivən〕*adv.* 甚至更 (用於比較級前面，加強語氣)

worse〔wɝs〕*adj.* 更糟的 (*bad* 的比較級)

usual〔'juʒʊəl〕*n.* 平常的

maybe〔'mebɪ〕*adv.* 大概；或許

accident〔'æksədənt〕*n.* 車禍

ahead〔ə'hɛd〕*adv.* 在前面

speaker〔'spikɚ〕*n.* 說話者

stuck〔stʌk〕*adj.* 卡住的；不能動彈的

leave〔liv〕*v.* 離開   ***on time*** 準時

30. (**A**) W: That's a fantastic coat you're wearing.

　　　　M: Thank you. It was a birthday present.

　　　　W: Well, it looks great.

　　　　M: So does your jacket. I love the color.

Question : What do we know from this conversation?

A. The man's jacket was a birthday present.

B. The woman will give the man a coat for his birthday.

C. The woman received a coat on her last birthday.

* fantastic〔fæn'tæstɪk〕*adj.* 很棒的（= *great*）
 coat〔kot〕*n.* 外套　　 wear〔wɛr〕*v.* 穿
 present〔'prɛzn̩t〕*n.* 禮物
 look〔lʊk〕*v.* 看起來　　 jacket〔'dʒækɪt〕*n.* 夾克
 So does your jacket. 你的夾克也是（看起來很棒）。
 color〔'kʌlɚ〕*n.* 顏色
 conversation〔͵kɑnvɚ'seʃən〕*n.* 對話
 receive〔rɪ'siv〕*v.* 收到　　 last〔læst〕*adj.* 上一個的

全民英語能力分級檢定測驗
初級測驗⑩

　　本測驗分三部份，全為三選一之選擇題，每部份各 10 題，共 30 題，作答時間約 20 分鐘。

第一部份：看圖辨義

　　　　本部份共 10 題，試題冊上每題有一個圖片，請聽錄音機 播出一個相關的問題，與 A、B、C 三個英語敘述後，選 一個與所看到圖片最相符的答案，並在答案紙上相對的圓 圈內塗黑作答。每題播出一遍，問題及選項均不印在試題 冊上。

例：（看）

（聽）

Look at the picture. How much is the hamburger?

A. It's eighty dollars.
B. It's fifty-five dollars.
C. It's eighteen dollars.

正確答案為 A

A. <u>Questions 1-2</u>

B. <u>Question 3</u>

C. <u>Questions 4-5</u>

D. <u>Question 6</u>

請 翻 頁 ⫸

E. Question 7

F. Question 8

G. **Question 9**

H. **Question 10**

Joyce's dinner

請 翻 頁 ⟾

第二部份: 問答

本部份共10題,每題錄音機會播出一個問句或直述句,
每題播出一次,聽後請從試題冊上 A、B、C 三個選項
中,選出一個最適合的回答或回應,並在答案紙上塗黑
作答。

例:

(聽) Good morning, Kevin. How are you?

(看) A. I'm fine, thank you.
B. I'm in the living room.
C. My name is Kevin.

正確答案為 A

11. A. I told you all that
studying would pay off.
B. Don't worry. You'll
do better next time.
C. When is the test?

12. A. He is absent today.
B. He is always late for
school.
C. He must be sick.

13. A. Yes, i do.
B. Yes, I think so.
C. No, it doesn't.

14. A. It really suits you.
B. Most children like
to color.
C. I don't have a
favorite color.

15. A. Let's listen to it again.
    B. You sing very well.
    C. It's mine, too.

16. A. I played basketball after school.
    B. There is a TV program I want to watch tonight.
    C. I used the break time to work on it.

17. A. We'll have to pull it out then.
    B. What did you eat today?
    C. Do you think it's broken?

18. A. That must have been expensive.
    B. You shouldn't spend so much time on the phone.
    C. What did you call her?

19. A. Yes, I have one.
    B. No, I have not.
    C. Yes, I haven't.

20. A. I was too busy.
    B. All right. I'd like that.
    C. Mary cannot come, either.

請 翻 頁 ⟹

第三部份: 簡短對話

　　　　本部份共 10 題,每題錄音機會播出一段對話及一個相關的問題,每題播出兩次,聽後請從試題冊上 A、B、C 三個選項中,選出一個最適合的回答,並在答案紙上塗黑作答。

例:

（聽）(Woman)　Good afternoon, …Mr. Davis?

　　　(Man)　　Yes.　I have an appointment with Dr. Sanders at two o'clock.　My son Tommy has a fever.

　　　(Woman)　Oh, that's too bad.　Well, please have a seat, Mr. Davis.　Dr. Sanders will be right with you.

　　　Question:　Where did this conversation take place?

（看）A.　In a post office.

　　　B.　In a restaurant.

　　　C.　In a doctor's office.

　　　正確答案爲 C

21. A. Thirsty.
    B. Tired.
    C. Hungry.

22. A. He wants to make
       sure his health is OK.
    B. He has an urgent
       medical problem.
    C. He wants to spend the
       morning with the
       doctor.

23. A. She often buys clothes
       for the woman.
    B. She is beautiful.
    C. She can sew very
       well.

24. A. In about three weeks.
    B. In the summer.
    C. For about three
       weeks.

25. A. Waiter and customer.
    B. Boss and employee.
    C. Host and guest.

26. A. She was driving too fast.
    B. She is not old enough to
       drive.
    C. Her car broke down.

27. A. His brother has about 20
       more cards.
    B. His brother has far more
       cards.
    C. The woman has the
       smallest number of cards.

28. A. She was stood up by her
       friend.
    B. She did not keep her
       appointment.
    C. She waited a long time.

29. A. He does not like shrimp.
    B. It would make him sick.
    C. It was not cooked well.

30. A. A box of books.
    B. An important letter.
    C. The woman's book.

請 翻 頁 ◖◗⟹

初級英語聽力檢定⑩詳解

一、聽力測驗

第一部份

For questions number 1 and 2, please look at picture A.

1. (**B**) Who is in the living room?
   A. Five people can sit on the sofa.
   B. No one.
   C. He is behind the sofa.

   * ***living room*** 客廳
     sofa〔'sofə〕*n.* 沙發
     behind〔bɪ'haɪnd〕*prep.* 在…後面

2. (**A**) Please look at picture A again. Where is the television?
   A. It's between the stereo and the sofa.
   B. It's in front of the window.
   C. It's on the carpet.

   * television〔'tɛlə,vɪʒən〕*n.* 電視機
     between〔bə'twin〕*prep.* 在…之間
     stereo〔'stɛrɪo〕*n.* 立體音響
     in front of 在…前面
     window〔'wɪndo〕*n.* 窗戶
     carpet〔'kɑrpɪt〕*n.* 地毯

For question number 3, please look at picture B.

3. (**B**) Where are the hot air balloons?

    A. They are filled with hot air.

    B. They are high in the air.

    C. No one is in the balloons.

    * air〔εr〕*n.* 空氣　　balloon〔bə'lun〕*n.* 汽球

    hot air balloon 熱汽球　　***be filled with*** 充滿

    in the air 在空中

For questions number 4 and 5, please look at picture C.

4. (**A**) What will Judy do after school on Wednesday?

    A. She'll play the guitar.

    B. She'll go swimming.

    C. She'll go skating.

    * ***after school*** 放學後　　play〔ple〕*v.* 演奏（樂器）

    guitar〔gɪ'tɑr〕*n.* 吉他　　swim〔swɪm〕*v.* 游泳

    go swimming 去游泳　　skate〔sket〕*v.* 溜冰

    go skating 去溜冰　　club〔klʌb〕*n.* 俱樂部；社團

5. (**B**) Please look at picture C again. What do most of Judy's activities involve?

    A. On the weekend.

    B. Sports.

    C. At her school.

    * activity〔æk'tɪvətɪ〕*n.* 活動　　involve〔ɪn'vɑlv〕*v.* 包含

    weekend〔'wik'ɛnd〕*n.* 週末　　sport〔sport〕*n.* 運動

For question number 6, please look at picture D.

6. (**A**) What are the children talking about?

    A. The fireworks.

    B. They are playing with firecrackers.

    C. They are playing with balloons.

    * ***talk about*** 談論   firework ('faɪr,wɜk) *n.* 煙火

    play with 玩   firecracker ('faɪr,krækə) *n.* 鞭炮

    balloon (bə'lun) *n.* 汽球

For question number 7, please look at picture E.

7. (**A**) How many sweaters is the man selling?

    A. He is selling many sweaters.

    B. He is selling them for $299.

    C. He sells them by shouting.

    * sweater ('swɛtə) *n.* 毛衣   sell (sɛl) *v.* 賣

    by* + *V-ing 藉由～（方法）   shout (ʃaʊt) *v.* 喊叫

For question number 8, please look at picture F.

8. (**A**) How do they make the scooters move?

    A. With their feet.

    B. In the park.

    C. They make them stop.

    * make (mek) *v.* 使   scooter ('skutə) *n.* 滑板車

    move (muv) *v.* 移動   feet (fit) *n.* 腳（foot 的複數形）

    stop (stɑp) *v.* 停止

For question number 9, please look at picture G.

9. (**C**) How many hot drinks are there?

      A. They are drinking coffee.

      B. They are in a coffee shop.

      C. There are two coffees.

      * drink〔drɪŋk〕*n.* 飲料　*v.* 喝　***hot drink*** 熱飲

        coffee〔'kɔfɪ〕*n.* 咖啡　***coffee shop*** 咖啡店

For question number 10, please look at picture H.

10. (**C**) What kind of food does Joyce like to eat?

      A. She can eat at McDonald's.

      B. She eats it for dinner.

      C. She likes fast food.

      * kind〔kaɪnd〕*n.* 種類　***fast food*** 速食

第二部份

11. (**B**) I'm really upset about my test score.

      A. I told you all that studying would pay off.

      B. Don't worry. You'll do better next time.

      C. When is the test?

      * upset〔ʌp'sɛt〕*adj.* 不高興的

        test〔tɛst〕*n.* 考試　score〔skor〕*n.* 成績

        pay off 划得來；有結果　worry〔'wʒɪ〕*v.* 擔心

        do better 考得比較好　***next time*** 下一次

12. (**C**) Why didn't John come to school today?

A. He is absent today.

B. He is always late for school.

C. He must be sick.

* absent〔'æbsn̩t〕*adj.* 缺席的

late〔let〕*adj.* 遲到的　　sick〔sɪk〕*adj.* 生病的

13. (**B**) Is it supposed to rain today?

A. Yes, I do.

B. Yes, I think so.

C. No, it doesn't.

* suppose〔sə'poz〕*v.* 猜想　　***be supposed to V.*** 應該~

rain〔ren〕*v.* 下雨

14. (**A**) What do you think of this color?

A. It really suits you.

B. Most children like to color.

C. I don't have a favorite color.

* ***think of*** 認為　　color〔'kʌlɚ〕*n.* 顏色　*v.* 著色

suit〔sut〕*v.* 適合　　favorite〔'fevərɪt〕*adj.* 最喜愛的

15. (**C**) Turn up the radio. This is my favorite song.

A. Let's listen to it again.

B. You sing very well.

C. It's mine, too.

* ***turn up*** （音量）轉大聲

radio〔'redɪ‚o〕*n.* 收音機　***listen to*** 聽

16. (**C**) How did you finish your homework so fast?

A. I played basketball after school.

B. There is a TV program I want to watch tonight.

C. I used the break time to work on it.

* finish〔'fɪnɪʃ〕 *v.* 完成　　homework〔'hom,wɜk〕 *n.* 功課

basketball〔'bæskɪt,bɔl〕 *n.* 籃球

program〔'progræm〕 *n.* 節目

break〔brek〕 *n.* 休息　　***work on*** 致力於

17. (**B**) Doctor, I have a terrible stomachache.

A. We'll have to pull it out then.

B. What did you eat today?

C. Do you think it's broken?

* terrible〔'tɛrəbḷ〕 *adj.* 嚴重的

stomachache〔'stʌmək,ek〕 *n.* 胃痛

pull out 拔出　　then〔ðɛn〕 *adv.* 那麼

broken〔'brokən〕 *adj.* 破碎的；損壞的

18. (**A**) My girlfriend called me long-distance on my birthday.

A. That must have been expensive.

B. You shouldn't spend so much time on the phone.

C. What did you call her?

* girlfriend〔'gɜl,frɛnd〕 *n.* 女朋友

call〔kɔl〕 *v.* 打電話給～；稱呼

long-distance〔'lɔŋ'dɪstəns〕 *adv.* 透過長途電話

must have + ***p.p.*** 當時一定～

expensive〔ɪk'spɛnsɪv〕 *adj.* 昂貴的

on the phone 講電話

19. (**B**) You haven't seen my pen anywhere, have you?

    A. Yes, I have one.   B. No, I have not.

    C. Yes, I haven't.

    * anywhere〔'ɛnɪˌhwɛr〕adv. 什麼地方也（不…）

    （用於否定句或疑問句）

20. (**B**) Why don't you come with us tomorrow?

    A. I was too busy.   B. All right. I'd like that.

    C. Mary cannot come, either.

    * *Why don't you~?* 你為何不~？（表提議）

    All right. 好。   either〔'iðɚ〕adv. 也（用於否定句）

第三部份

21. (**B**) W: How was your trip?

    M: It was long and uncomfortable. But I'm glad to be here.

    W: Let's go home so that you can take a rest.

    Question: How does the man feel after his trip?

    A. Thirsty.   B. Tired.

    C. Hungry.

    * trip〔trɪp〕n. 旅行

    uncomfortable〔ʌn'kʌmfɚtəbl̩〕adj. 不舒服的

    glad〔glæd〕adj. 高興的   *so that* 以便於（表目的）

    rest〔rɛst〕n. 休息   *take a rest* 休息

    thirsty〔'θɝstɪ〕adj. 口渴的   tired〔taɪrd〕adj. 疲倦的

    hungry〔'hʌŋgrɪ〕adj. 飢餓的

22. (**A**) M : Good morning. I'd like to make an appointment
              for a checkup.

         W : Very well. The doctor can see you tomorrow at
               3:00.

         M : I'm sorry. I can't come then.

         W : How about next week? There is an opening on
               Tuesday morning.

         M : That will be fine.

         Question : Why does the man want to see the doctor?

      A. He wants to make sure his health is OK.

      B. He has an urgent medical problem.

      C. He wants to spend the morning with the doctor.

* ***would like to V.*** 想要（**＝** *want to V.*）

     appointment（ ə'pɔɪntmənt ）*n.* 約會

     checkup（'tʃɛk‚ʌp ）*n.* 健康檢查

     Very well. 好的。   sorry（'sɔrɪ ）*adj.* 抱歉的

     then（ ðɛn ）*adv.* 那時   ***How about~?*** ～如何？

     opening（'opənɪŋ ）*n.* 空缺   fine（ faɪn ）*adj.* 沒問題的

     make sure 確定   health（ hɛlθ ）*n.* 健康

     OK 沒問題的（ ＝ *all right*）

     urgent（'ɝdʒənt ）*adj.* 緊急的

     medical（'mɛdɪkḷ ）*adj.* 醫療的

     problem（'prɑbləm ）*n.* 問題

     spend（ spɛnd ）*v.* 渡過（時間）

23. (**C**) M: That's a beautiful dress.

W: Thank you. My sister made it.

M: Wow. She's really talented.

W: Yeah. She wants to be a designer someday.

Question : What do we know about the woman's sister?

A. She often buys clothes for the woman.

B. She is beautiful.　　C. She can sew very well.

* beautiful〔'bjutəfəl〕 *adj.* 漂亮的

　 dress〔drɛs〕 *n.* 洋裝　　make〔mek〕 *v.* 做

　 wow〔waʊ〕 *interj.* 哇！噢！（表示驚訝等的叫聲）

　 talented〔'tæləntɪd〕 *adj.* 有天賦的；有才華的

　 yeah〔jɛ〕 *adv.* 是的（＝*yes*）

　 designer〔dɪ'zaɪnɚ〕 *n.* （時裝）設計師

　 someday〔'sʌm,de〕 *adv.* 將來有一天　　sew〔so〕 *v.* 縫紉

24. (**B**) W: Have you ever been to France?

M: Not yet. But my family and I will go this summer.

W: Really? That's so exciting. How long will you stay?

M: About three weeks.

Question : When will the man visit France?

A. In about three weeks.　　B. In the summer.

C. For about three weeks.

* *have been to* 曾經去過　　ever〔'ɛvɚ〕 *adv.* 曾經

　 France〔fræns〕 *n.* 法國　　*not yet* 還沒

　 exciting〔ɪk'saɪtɪŋ〕 *adj.* 令人興奮的

　 How long~? ～多久？　　stay〔ste〕 *v.* 停留

　 visit〔'vɪzɪt〕 *v.* 參觀；遊覽

　 in about three weeks 大約再過三個星期

25. (**C**) M: Would you like some more?

W: No, I couldn't. I'm stuffed. But everything was delicious.

M: Well, I'm glad you enjoyed it.

W: I had no idea you were such a fantastic cook.

Question : What is the relationship between the speakers?

A. Waiter and customer.

B. Boss and employee.

C. Host and guest.

* stuffed〔stʌft〕adj. 吃得飽的

delicious〔dɪ'lɪʃəs〕adj. 好吃的

enjoy〔ɪn'dʒɔɪ〕v. 喜歡　　**have no idea** 不知道

such〔sʌtʃ〕adj. 這樣的（加強語氣）

fantastic〔fæn'tæstɪk〕adj. 極好的；了不起的

cook〔kʊk〕n. 廚師

relationship〔rɪ'leʃən,ʃɪp〕n. 關係

speaker〔'spikɚ〕n. 說話者　　waiter〔'wetɚ〕n. 服務生

customer〔'kʌstəmɚ〕n. 顧客　　boss〔bɔs〕n. 老板

employee〔,ɛmplɔɪ'i〕n. 員工　　host〔host〕n. 主人

guest〔gɛst〕n. 客人

26. (**A**)　M : May I see your license, please?

W : Um, I, uh, I don't have it, officer.

M : Why not?

W : I must have left it at home. I'm really sorry.

M : Well, I'm going to have to write you two tickets. One for speeding and one for not carrying your license.

Question : Why did the police officer stop the woman?

A. She was driving too fast.

B. She is not old enough to drive.

C. Her car broke down.

* license〔ˈlaɪsn̩s〕*n.* 執照（這裡是指 driver's license「駕駛執照」）

officer〔ˈɔfəsɚ〕*n.* 警察（= *police officer*）

leave〔liv〕*v.* 遺留　　write〔raɪt〕*v.* 開（罰單）

ticket〔ˈtɪkɪt〕*n.* 罰單　　speed〔spid〕*v.* 超速

carry〔ˈkærɪ〕*v.* 攜帶　　stop〔stɑp〕*v.* 攔下

drive〔draɪv〕*v.* 駕駛（汽車等）　　***break down*** 拋錨

27. (**B**)　W : How many cards have you collected?

M : Forty-three.

W : Wow. I only have about 20.

M : This is nothing. My brother has over 100.

Question : How does the man's collection compare to that of his brother?

A. His brother has about 20 more cards

B. His brother has far more cards.

C. The woman has the smallest number of cards.

* card〔kɑrd〕*n.* 卡片　　collect〔kə'lɛkt〕*v.* 收集
  over〔'ovɚ〕*prep.* 超過 (= *more than*)
  collection〔kə'lɛkʃən〕*n.* 收藏品
  compare〔kəm'pɛr〕*v.* 比較 < *to* >
  that 在此代替 the collection，避免重複。
  far〔fɑr〕*adv.* 很 (修飾比較級，加強語氣)
  number〔'nʌmbɚ〕*n.* 數量

28. (**B**)　W: You look upset.　What's wrong?

M: Joan was supposed to meet me here, but she stood me up!

W: I'm sure she didn't mean to.　Maybe she got caught in traffic.

M: You're right.　I'll wait a little longer.

Question : What happened to Joan?

A. She was stood up by her friend.

B. She did not keep her appointment.

C. She waited a long time.

* look〔luk〕*v.* 看起來
  What's wrong? 怎麼了？ (= *What's the matter?*)
  meet〔mit〕*v.* 和～碰面　　***stand sb. up*** 放某人鴿子
  sure〔ʃur〕*adj.* 確定的　　mean〔min〕*v.* 意圖；有意
  maybe〔'mebɪ〕*adv.* 大概；或許　　***get caught*** 受困
  traffic〔'træfɪk〕*n.* 交通；(往來的) 車輛
  wait〔wet〕*v.* 等待　　***a little*** 一點
  sb. happen to sb. 某人發生某事
  keep〔kip〕*v.* 履行；遵守
  keep one's appointment 準時赴約

29. (**B**) M: Waitress, can you tell me what is in this dish?

W: Sure. Fish, vegetables, shrimp…

M: Oh! I'm allergic to shrimp. I can't eat it or I'll
get sick.

W: I'm sorry. I'll bring you something else.

Question : Why doesn't the man want to eat the dish?

A. He does not like shrimp.

B. It would make him sick.   C. It was not cooked well.

* waitress〔'wetrɪs〕*n.* 女服務生   dish〔dɪʃ〕*n.* 菜餚
  sure〔ʃur〕*adv.* 當然   fish〔fɪʃ〕*n.* 魚
  vegetable〔'vɛdʒətəbḷ〕*n.* 蔬菜   shrimp〔ʃrɪmp〕*n.* 蝦子
  allergic〔ə'lɝdʒɪk〕*adj.* 過敏的 < *to* >
  or〔ɔr〕*conj.* 否則;要不然
  sick〔sɪk〕*adj.* 生病的;覺得噁心的
  else〔ɛls〕*adj.* 其他的   cook〔kuk〕*v.* 烹煮

30. (**A**) W: A package arrived for you today.

M: Oh, it must be the books I ordered.

W: I put it on your desk.

M: Thank you.

Question : What is on the man's desk?

A. A box of books.   B. An important letter.

C. The woman's book.

* package〔'pækɪdʒ〕*n.* 包裹
  arrive〔ə'raɪv〕*v.* (郵件、物品等) 被送來
  order〔'ɔrdɚ〕*v.* 訂購   put〔put〕*v.* 放
  box〔baks〕*n.* (一) 箱
  important〔ɪm'pɔrtṇt〕*adj.* 重要的   letter〔'lɛtɚ〕*n.* 信件

全民英語能力分級檢定測驗
初級測驗⑪

本測驗分三部份，全為三選一之選擇題，每部份各 10 題，共 30 題，作答時間約 20 分鐘。

第一部份：看圖辨義

本部份共 10 題，試題冊上每題有一個圖片，請聽錄音機播出一個相關的問題，與 A、B、C 三個英語敘述後，選一個與所看到圖片最相符的答案，並在答案紙上相對的圓圈內塗黑作答。每題播出一遍，問題及選項均不印在試題冊上。

例：（看）

NT$80

NT$50

（聽）

Look at the picture. How much is the hamburger?

A. It's eighty dollars.
B. It's fifty-five dollars.
C. It's eighteen dollars.

正確答案為 A

A. **Questions 1-2**

B. **Question 3**

C. Questions 4-5

John   May   Steve

D. Question 6

請翻頁 ▯⟹

E. **Question 7**

F. **Question 8**

G. **Question 9**

H. **Question 10**

請翻頁 ⬜⟹

第二部份： 問答

　　　本部份共 10 題，每題錄音機會播出一個問句或直述句，
　　　每題播出一次，聽後請從試題冊上 A、B、C 三個選項
　　　中，選出一個最適合的回答或回應，並在答案紙上塗黑
　　　作答。

例：

　（聽）　Good morning, Kevin. How are you?

　（看）　A.　I'm fine, thank you.
　　　　　B.　I'm in the living room.
　　　　　C.　My name is Kevin.

　　　　　正確答案為 A

11. A. Where? I don't see her.
　　B. All right. See you then.
　　C. Sure, she studies hard.

12. A. No. My brother is not
　　　　that tall.
　　B. Yes, he can play very
　　　　well.
　　C. No. She is in school
　　　　now.

13. A. She is sixteen.
　　B. She is at home.
　　C. She's much better,
　　　　thanks.

14. A. I do, too.
　　B. I'd love to go.
　　C. Mine, too.

15. A. Don't worry. She is always late.

    B. I got a letter from her yesterday.

    C. Yes, I've heard of her.

16. A. Why don't you try on a smaller one?

    B. Let's go to Macy's. There is a sale.

    C. I'm sorry you don't like it.

17. A. Oh! You shouldn't have.

    B. Don't mention it.

    C. Thank you so much.

18. A. Yes, I did. Why?

    B. No, I did lock it.

    C. Yes, I never lock the door.

19. A. I slept late last night.

    B. I stayed up too late last night.

    C. I slept in this morning.

20. A. It's delicious.

    B. Cake is my favorite dessert.

    C. I think it's your birthday.

請 翻 頁 ▷

第三部份： 簡短對話

本部份共 10 題，每題錄音機會播出一段對話及一個相關
的問題，每題播出兩次，聽後請從試題冊上 A、B、C 三
個選項中，選出一個最適合的回答，並在答案紙上塗黑
作答。

例：

（聽）(Woman) Good afternoon, ...Mr. Davis?

(Man) Yes. I have an appointment with
Dr. Sanders at two o'clock. My
son Tommy has a fever.

(Woman) Oh, that's too bad. Well, please
have a seat, Mr. Davis. Dr.
Sanders will be right with you.

Question: Where did this conversation take
place?

（看）A. In a post office.

B. In a restaurant.

C. In a doctor's office.

正確答案爲 C

21. A. It is too dangerous to fly during the storm.
    B. He arrived at the airport too late.
    C. The airline no longer flies to New York.

22. A. She sometimes watches TV and sometimes reads newspapers.
    B. She usually watches TV and seldom reads a newspaper.
    C. She always watches TV if she doesn't read a newspaper.

23. A. Look for their dog in the park.
    B. Go to a movie about dogs.
    C. Watch some dogs compete for prizes.

24. A. He did not finish his homework.
    B. He woke up too late and missed the test.
    C. He does not feel well.

25. A. A doctor.
    B. A veterinarian.
    C. A mechanic.

26. A. A hotel room.
    B. An airline ticket.
    C. A table at a restaurant.

請 翻 頁 ◀▭⟹

27. A. The woman failed the
   chemistry exam
   because she did not
   study hard enough.

   B. The woman thinks she
   would have done better
   if she had studied for
   four hours.

   C. The man spent twice
   as long studying for the
   chemistry exam than
   the woman.

28. A. Fifteen thousand.
   B. Fifty thousand.
   C. Hundreds of thousands.

29. A. Sally introduced
   John and Sarah.

   B. Sally often talked to
   John about Sarah.

   C. Sarah has wanted to
   meet John for a long
   time.

30. A. There is only one
   more.

   B. There are no more.

   C. All the cans are
   there except for the
   last one.

初級英語聽力檢定⑪詳解

第一部份

For questions number 1 and 2, please look at picture A.

1. (**B**) How many drawers are there in the desk?
   A. Yes, it is a drawing of a desk.
   B. There are three.
   C. There is a cat.

   * *How many~?* ～多少？　　drawer〔`drɔr`〕*n.* 抽屜
     drawing〔`'drɔ‧ɪŋ`〕*n.* 圖畫

2. (**A**) Please look at picture A again. Where is the cat?
   A. It's under the desk.
   B. It's on the desk.
   C. It's in the drawer.

   * under〔`'ʌndɚ`〕*prep.* 在…下面

For question number 3, please look at picture B.

3. (**B**) Who has more pens?
   A. Most of the pens are in the cup.
   B. Sandy does.
   C. They belong to Candy.

   * cup〔`kʌp`〕*n.* 杯子
     Sandy does. 珊蒂有比較多支筆。(= *Sandy has more pens.*)
     belong to 屬於

For questions number 4 and 5, please look at picture C.

4.(**C**) Who wears a beard?

        A. John.

        B. May.

        C. Steve.

        * wear〔wɛr〕*v.* 留（鬍子）　　beard〔bɪrd〕*n.* 鬍子

5.(**B**) Please look at picture C again. Who is on May's right?

        A. It's on her leg.

        B. John is.

        C. The man with a pair of glasses.

        * right〔raɪt〕*n.* 右邊

          on** one's **right 在某人的右邊

          leg〔lɛg〕*n.* 腿　　***a pair of*** 一副

          glasses〔'glæsɪz〕*n. pl.* 眼鏡

For question number 6, please look at picture D.

6.(**C**) Who is getting into the taxi?

        A. The driver.

        B. Through the door.

        C. The passenger.

        * ***get into*** 上（車）　　taxi〔'tæksɪ〕*n.* 計程車

          driver〔'draɪvɚ〕*n.* 司機

          through〔θru〕*prep.* 通過；穿過

          passenger〔'pæsṇdʒɚ〕*n.* 乘客

For question number 7, please look at picture E.

7. (**C**) What is he delivering?

    A. He is the mailman.

    B. In the mailbox.

    C. Some letters.

    * deliver〔dɪ'lɪvɚ〕*v.* 遞送

      mailman〔'mel,mæn〕*n.* 郵差

      mailbox〔'mel,bɑks〕*n.* 信箱   letter〔'lɛtɚ〕*n.* 信件

For question number 8, please look at picture F.

8. (**A**) What can you buy in the last store on the right?

    A. Shoes and boots.

    B. It is the computer store.

    C. You can buy a book.

    * last〔læst〕*adj.* 最後的   ***on the right*** 在右邊

      shoes〔ʃuz〕*n. pl.* 鞋子   boots〔buts〕*n. pl.* 靴子

      computer〔kəm'pjutɚ〕*n.* 電腦

For question number 9, please look at picture G.

9. (**C**) Where is the car?

    A. The car is in the garage.

    B. It's a garbage truck.

    C. The car is parked in front of the garage.

    * garage〔gə'rɑʒ〕*n.* 車庫   garbage〔'gɑrbɪdʒ〕*n.* 垃圾

      truck〔trʌk〕*n.* 卡車   ***garbage truck*** 垃圾車

      park〔pɑrk〕*v.* 停（車）   ***in front of*** 在…前面

For question number 10, please look at picture H.

10. (**B**) What does the woman want to do?

    A. Cross the street.   B. Catch a bus.

    C. Drive a bus.

    * cross〔krɔs〕v. 穿越   catch〔kætʃ〕v. 趕上

    drive〔draɪv〕v. 駕駛（汽車）

第二部份

11. (**C**) I see Penny at the library every night.

    A. Where? I don't see her.

    B. All right. See you then.

    C. Sure, she studies hard.

    * library〔'laɪˌbrɛrɪ〕n. 圖書館   ***All right***. 好。

    See you then. 到時候見。   sure〔ʃur〕adv. 當然

    study〔'stʌdɪ〕v. 讀書   hard〔hɑrd〕adv. 努力地

12. (**A**) Is that your brother on the basketball court?

    A. No. My brother is not that tall.

    B. Yes, he can play very well.

    C. No. She is in school now.

    * basketball〔'bæskɪtˌbɔl〕n. 籃球

    court〔kort〕n.（籃球等的）球場   that〔ðæt〕adv. 那樣

13. (**C**) How is your sister now?

    A. She is sixteen.   B. She is at home.

    C. She's much better, thanks.

14. (**C**) Swimming is my favorite sport.

      A. I do, too.   B. I'd love to go.

      C. Mine, too.

    * swimming〔'swɪmɪŋ〕*n.* 游泳

      favorite〔'fevərɪt〕*adj.* 最喜愛的   sport〔sport〕*n.* 運動

      would love to V. 想要 (= *would like to V.*)

      mine〔maɪn〕*pron.* I 的所有代名詞;我的東西 (在此等於

        my favorite sport)

15. (**B**) Have you heard from Joan lately?

      A. Don't worry. She is always late.

      B. I got a letter from her yesterday.

      C. Yes, I've heard of her.

    * ***hear from sb.*** 得到某人的消息;接到某人的來信

      lately〔'letlɪ〕*adv.* 最近   worry〔'wɝɪ〕*v.* 擔心

      always〔'ɔlwez〕*adv.* 總是   late〔let〕*adj.* 遲的

      hear of 聽說過

16. (**B**) This jacket is too expensive for me.

      A. Why don't you try on a smaller one?

      B. Let's go to Macy's. There is a sale.

      C. I'm sorry you don't like it.

    * jacket〔'dʒækɪt〕*n.* 夾克

      expensive〔ɪk'spɛnsɪv〕*adj.* 昂貴的

      Why don't you ~ ? 你爲何不 ~ ? (表提議)

      try on 試穿   ***Macy's*** 梅西百貨公司

      sale〔sel〕*n.* 拍賣   sorry〔'sɔrɪ〕*adj.* 遺憾的;道歉的

17. (**C**) Excuse me. You dropped this.

A. Oh! You shouldn't have.

B. Don't mention it.　　C. Thank you so much.

* *excuse me* 對不起　　drop〔drɑp〕*v.* 掉落
You shouldn't have. 你不用這麼做的；你太客氣了。
Don't mention it. 不客氣。

18. (**A**) You didn't lock the door, did you?

A. Yes, I did. Why?　　B. No, I did lock it.

C. Yes, I never lock the door.

* lock〔lɑk〕*v.* 鎖
B. did 表「真的」，在此加強語氣用，等於 really。

19. (**B**) Why are you so tired today?

A. I slept late last night.

B. I stayed up too late last night.

C. I slept in this morning.

* tired〔taɪrd〕*adj.* 疲累的　　sleep〔slip〕*v.* 睡覺（三態變化
為：sleep-slept-slept）　　late〔let〕*adv.* 晚
I slept late last night. 我昨晚很晚睡。　　*stay up* 熬夜
sleep in 早上起得晚；睡過頭

20. (**A**) What do you think of this cake?

A. It's delicious.　　B. Cake is my favorite dessert.

C. I think it's your birthday.

* *think of* 認為　　cake〔kek〕*n.* 蛋糕
delicious〔dɪ'lɪʃəs〕*adj.* 好吃的
dessert〔dɪ'zɝt〕*n.* 甜點

第三部份

21. (**A**) W: I'm sorry, sir. That flight has been cancelled.

M: Can you put me on another flight?

W: Not until tomorrow, and then only if the weather improves.

M: That's terrible. I'll be late for my meeting in New York.

Question: Why was the man's flight cancelled?

A. It is too dangerous to fly during the storm.

B. He arrived at the airport too late.

C. The airline no longer flies to New York.

* sir〔sɝ〕n. 先生　　flight〔flaɪt〕n. 班機
cancel〔'kænsl〕v. 取消
put me on another flight 讓我搭另一班飛機
not until 直到…才～　　then〔ðɛn〕adv. 此外；還有
weather〔'wɛðɚ〕n. 天氣　　improve〔ɪm'pruv〕v. 改善
terrible〔'tɛrəbl〕adj. 糟糕的
meeting〔'mitɪŋ〕n. 會議　　***New York*** 紐約
dangerous〔'dendʒərəs〕adj. 危險的
fly〔flaɪ〕v. 搭飛機　　during〔'djʊrɪŋ〕prep. 在…期間
storm〔stɔrm〕n. 暴風雨　　arrive〔ə'raɪv〕v. 到達
airport〔'ɛr,port〕n. 機場
airline〔'ɛr,laɪn〕n.（飛機的）航線；航空公司
no longer 不再

22.(**B**) M: Did you read the newspaper today?

W: No. I rarely read one.

M: Then how do you know what has happened?

W: I just watch the news on TV.

Question : Which of the following is true about the
woman?

A. She sometimes watches TV and sometimes reads
newspapers.

B. She usually watches TV and seldom reads a
newspaper.

C. She always watches TV if she doesn't read a
newspaper.

* newspaper (ˈnjuzˌpepɚ) *n.* 報紙
  rarely (ˈrɛrlɪ) *adv.* 很少 (= seldom (ˈsɛldəm))
  happen (ˈhæpən) *v.* 發生　　just (dʒʌst) *adv.* 只是
  news (njuz) *n.* 新聞　　following (ˈfɑləwɪŋ) *adj.* 下列的
  true (tru) *adj.* 眞實的；正確的
  sometimes (ˈsʌmˌtaɪmz) *adv.* 有時
  usually (ˈjuʒʊəlɪ) *adv.* 通常

23.(**C**) M: Are you a dog lover?

W: I sure am. Why?

M: There's a dog show at the park this Sunday. Do
you want to go?

W: I'd love to. We should see some real champions
there.

Question : What are the speakers going to do on Sunday?

A: Look for their dog in the park.

B. Go to a movie about dogs.

C. Watch some dogs compete for prizes.

* lover ('lʌvɚ) *n.* 愛好者   show (ʃo) *n.* 展覽；表演
  champion ('tʃæmpɪən) *n.* 冠軍；優於其他者的人或動物
  speaker ('spikɚ) *n.* 說話者   *look for* 尋找
  go to a movie 去看電影   compete (kəm'pit) *v.* 競賽
  prize (praɪz) *n.* 獎品；獎金

24. (**C**) M: Mom, can I stay home from school today?

   W: Why? What's wrong with you?

   M: I stayed up late studying for the test and now I have
     a headache and sore throat.

   W: You know you shouldn't stay up. It's bad for your
     health.

   Question : Why does the boy want to stay home?

   A. He did not finish his homework.

   B. He woke up too late and missed the test.

   C. He does not feel well.

   * *What's wrong with ~ ?* ～怎麼了？(= *What's the matter*
     with ~ ?)   test (tɛst) *n.* 考試
     headache ('hɛd,ek) *n.* 頭痛   sore (sor) *adj.* 疼痛的
     throat (θrot) *n.* 喉嚨   *have a sore throat* 喉嚨痛
     health (hɛlθ) *n.* 健康   finish ('fɪnɪʃ) *v.* 完成
     homework ('hom,wɝk) *n.* 家庭作業   *wake up* 醒過來
     miss (mɪs) *v.* 錯過   well (wɛl) *adj.* 身體健康的

25. (**C**)　M : What seems to be the problem?

W : Well, it just stopped in the middle of the road.

M : You mean the engine died?

W : Yeah. And I couldn't get it started again.

Question : Who is the man?

A. A doctor.　　　　　B. A veterinarian.

C. A mechanic.

* seem〔sim〕v. 看來；似乎　problem〔'prɑbləm〕n. 問題

stop〔stɑp〕v. 停止　middle〔'mɪdl〕n. 中央

mean〔min〕v. 意思是　engine〔'ɛndʒən〕n. 引擎

die〔daɪ〕v.（機器）突然停止運轉

yeah〔jɛ〕adv. 是的（= yes）　get〔gɛt〕v. 使

start〔stɑrt〕v. 啓動

veterinarian〔,vɛtərə'nɛrɪən〕n. 獸醫（= vet）

mechanic〔mə'kænɪk〕n. 技工

26. (**C**)　W : I'd like to make a reservation for the 26th.

M : Of course. For what time?

W : Eight o'clock.

M : And for how many people?

W : Two.

Question : What is the woman reserving?

A. A hotel room.　　　B. An airline ticket.

C. A table at a restaurant.

* reservation〔,rɛzə'veʃən〕n. 預訂　*of course* 當然

reserve〔rɪ'zɝv〕v. 預訂　hotel〔ho'tɛl〕n. 旅館

airline ticket 機票　restaurant〔'rɛstərənt〕n. 餐廳

27. (**B**) M : How did you do in the chemistry exam?

W : Not bad. But I don't think I studied hard enough.

M : How much time did you spend on it?

W : About two hours, but I should have studied for twice that long.

Question : Which of the following statements is correct?

A. The woman failed the chemistry exam because she did not study hard enough.

B. The woman thinks she would have done better if she had studied for four hours.

C. The man spent twice as long studying for the chemistry exam than the woman.

* chemistry ('kɛmɪstrɪ) n. 化學

   exam (ɪg'zæm) n. 考試

   spend (spɛnd) v. 花 (時間) < on >

   should have + ***p.p.*** 當初應該 (表過去該做而未做)

   twice (twaɪs) adv. 兩倍

   statement ('stetmənt) n. 陳述；說明

   correct (kə'rɛkt) adj. 正確的

   fail (fel) v. (考試) 不合格

28. (**A**)　W: Look at the crowd of people! There must be
　　　　　　　　thousands there.

　　　　　　M: Sure. The stadium has 15,000 seats.

　　　　　　W: Wow. And it looks full, too.

　　　　　　M: Well, this is an important game.

　　　　　　Question : How many people can go to a game at the
　　　　　　　　　　　　stadium?
　　　　　　A. Fifteen thousand.
　　　　　　B. Fifty thousand.
　　　　　　C. Hundreds of thousands.

　　　* crowd〔kraud〕n. 人群
　　　　　thousands〔'θauzṇdz〕n. pl. 數千
　　　　　stadium〔'stediəm〕n. 體育場　　　seat〔sit〕n. 座位
　　　　　wow〔wau〕interj. 哇！；噢！(表示驚訝等的叫聲)
　　　　　look〔luk〕v. 看起來　　　full〔ful〕adj. 滿的
　　　　　important〔ım'pɔrtṇt〕adj. 重要的
　　　　　game〔gem〕n. 比賽　　　*How many ~ ?*　~多少？
　　　　　fifteen thousand　一萬五千
　　　　　fifty thousand　五萬
　　　　　hundreds of thousands　數十萬

29. (**B**)　M: Excuse me. Aren't you Sarah, Sally's friend?

　　　　　　W: Yes, I am.

　　　　　　M: I'm John. Sally has told me a lot about you. It's
　　　　　　　　nice to finally meet you.

　　　　　　W: Nice to meet you, too, John.

Question : Which of the following statements is correct?

A. Sally introduced John and Sarah.

B. Sally often talked to John about Sarah.

C. Sarah has wanted to meet John for a long time.

* **a lot** 許多　　nice〔naɪs〕*adj.* 好的
  finally〔'faɪnḷɪ〕*adv.* 最後；終於
  meet〔mit〕*v.* 遇見；認識
  Nice to meet you. 很高興認識你。
  introduce〔ˌɪntrə'djus〕*v.* 介紹
  for a long time 很長一段時間

30. (**B**)　W : Are we out of soda?

M : No, there should be some in the refrigerator.

W : Oh, I see it. I'm taking the last one.

M : OK. I'll buy some more tomorrow.

Question : How many cans of soda are in the
　　　　　refrigerator after this conversation?

A. There is only one more.　　B. There are no more.

C. All the cans are there except for the last one.

* **be out of** 用完　　soda〔'sodə〕*n.* 汽水
  refrigerator〔rɪ'frɪdʒəˌretə〕*n.* 冰箱
  take〔tek〕*v.* 拿走　　last〔læst〕*adj.* 最後的
  OK. 好；沒問題。　　can〔kæn〕*n.* 罐頭
  conversation〔ˌkɑnvə'seʃən〕*n.* 對話
  except for 除了…以外

心得筆記欄

全民英語能力分級檢定測驗
初級測驗⑫

　　本測驗分三部份，全爲三選一之選擇題，每部份各 10 題，共 30 題，作答時間約 20 分鐘。

第一部份：看圖辨義

　　　　本部份共 10 題，試題冊上每題有一個圖片，請聽錄音機播出一個相關的問題，與 A、B、C 三個英語敘述後，選一個與所看到圖片最相符的答案，並在答案紙上相對的圓圈內塗黑作答。每題播出一遍，問題及選項均不印在試題冊上。

例：（看）

NT$80　　NT$50

（聽）

Look at the picture.　How much is the hamburger?

　　A. It's eighty dollars.
　　B. It's fifty-five dollars.
　　C. It's eighteen dollars.

正確答案爲 A

A. **Questions 1-2**

B. **Question 3**

Betty

C. **Questions 4-5**

D. **Question 6**

請翻頁 ⟹

E. **Question 7**

F. **Question 8**

G. **Question 9**

H. **Question 10**

請翻頁 ▭⇒

第二部份: 問答

本部份共 10 題,每題錄音機會播出一個問句或直述句,每題播出一次,聽後請從試題冊上 A、B、C 三個選項中,選出一個最適合的回答或回應,並在答案紙上塗黑作答。

例:

(聽) Good morning, Kevin. How are you?

(看) A. I'm fine, thank you.
　　　B. I'm in the living room.
　　　C. My name is Kevin.

正確答案為 A

11. A. It's beautiful.
　　 B. You didn't have to bring a gift!
　　 C. Thank you. I must have dropped it.

12. A. Chapter three.
　　 B. Ninety-seven.
　　 C. In the textbook.

13. A. I'd like chocolate, please.
　　 B. Two scoops, please.
　　 C. It's fifty dollars.

14. A. Yes.
　　 B. Yes, it's going to Keelung.
　　 C. About six o'clock.

15. A. I'll do that.
    B. I'll give it to you
       when I'm finished
       with it.
    C. Here you are.

16. A. I think so.
    B. I will buy it later.
    C. Yes, I can.

17. A. Yes, I see it over
       there.
    B. You had better
       close the window.
    C. Yes, it's a lovely day.

18. A. I thought the paintings
       were wonderful.
    B. They are a little too
       tight.
    C. It's on the second floor.

19. A. Nice to meet you, too.
    B. You're too kind.
    C. Your performance was
       wonderful.

20. A. No, you weren't.
    B. Yes, but the pool is
       closed.
    C. Yes, I'd love to go
       swimming.

請 翻 頁 ⟹

第三部份： 簡短對話

　　　　本部份共 10 題，每題錄音機會播出一段對話及一個相關的問題，每題播出兩次，聽後請從試題冊上 A、B、C 三個選項中，選出一個最適合的回答，並在答案紙上塗黑作答。

　　　　例：

（聽）(Woman)　　Good afternoon, …Mr. Davis?

　　　(Man)　　　Yes.　I have an appointment with Dr. Sanders at two o'clock.　My son Tommy has a fever.

　　　(Woman)　　Oh, that's too bad.　Well, please have a seat, Mr. Davis.　Dr. Sanders will be right with you.

　　　Question:　Where did this conversation take place?

（看）A.　In a post office.

　　　B.　In a restaurant.

　　　C.　In a doctor's office.

　　　　正確答案為 C

21. A. They will go another
       day.
    B. They will do
       something else.
    C. They will see a
       different movie.

22. A. She does not speak
       clearly.
    B. She speaks too softly.
    C. She does not
       understand English
       well.

23. A. He hopes to win the
       lottery.
    B. He hopes to go to
       NTU.
    C. He hopes Jerry is
       lucky at NTU.

24. A. She will choose the
       job.
    B. She will hear some
       good news.
    C. She will know
       whether she got the
       job.

25. A. He walked too
       slowly.
    B. We don't know.
    C. He missed the bus.

26. A. He thinks it will
       probably rain.
    B. He thinks it would be
       wrong not to take an
       umbrella.
    C. He thinks it is
       probably wrong.

請 翻 頁 ◖▢⟹

27. A. A choice of French
       fries or rice.
    B. Rice and a salad.
    C. Rice, and French fries
       or a salad.

28. A. Something that is in
       chapter seven might
       be on the test.
    B. The new formulas
       will not be on the test.
    C. The new formulas
       can be found in
       chapter eight.

29. A. He is a big Dragons
       fan.
    B. The Lions are not
       playing today.
    C. He prefers them to
       the Lions.

30. A. He said he didn't
       study enough.
    B. He said it was too
       hard.
    C. He said it was pretty
       easy.

初級英語聽力檢定⑫詳解

一、聽力測驗

第一部份

For questions number 1 and 2, please look at picture A.

1. (**B**) What are the three women doing?
   A. She is complaining about their food.
   B. They are ordering some food.
   C. They are inviting the man to have dinner.

   * complain〔kəm'plen〕v. 抱怨 < *about* >
     order〔'ɔrdə〕v. 點（餐）　　invite〔ɪn'vaɪt〕v. 邀請

2. (**C**) Please look at picture A again.　What does the man do?
   A. He's a cook.　　　　B. He's a writer.
   C. He's a waiter.

   * **What does** sb. **do?** 某人從事什麼工作？
     cook〔kʊk〕n. 廚師　　writer〔'raɪtə〕n. 作家
     waiter〔'wetə〕n. 服務生

For question number 3, please look at picture B.

3. (**A**) What is Betty singing?
   A. A song.　　　　B. On the stage.
   C. With a microphone.

   * stage〔stedʒ〕n. 舞台
     microphone〔'maɪkrə,fon〕n. 麥克風

For questions number 4 and 5, please look at picture C.

4. (**B**) What is the woman standing behind the chair?

        A. She's a singer.   B. She's a hairdresser.

        C. She's a dentist.

        * behind〔bɪˈhaɪnd〕*prep.* 在…的後面

           singer〔ˈsɪŋɚ〕*n.* 歌手

           hairdresser〔ˈhɛrˌdrɛsɚ〕*n.* 美髮師

           dentist〔ˈdɛntɪst〕*n.* 牙醫

5. (**A**) Please look at picture C again. What will the woman standing behind the chair do for the girl in the chair?

        A. Cut her hair.   B. Wash her face.

        C. Clean her teeth.

        * cut〔kʌt〕*v.* 剪   hair〔hɛr〕*n.* 頭髮

           wash〔wɑʃ〕*v.* 洗   face〔fes〕*n.* 臉

           clean〔klin〕*v.* 把…弄乾淨

           teeth〔tiθ〕*n. pl.* 牙齒（tooth 的複數形）

For question number 6, please look at picture D.

6. (**A**) It is now ten to eleven. Which movie can they see first?

        A. They can see *Cats & Dogs*.

        B. They can see *Without Love*.

        C. They can see either movie.

        * ***It's now ten to eleven.*** 現在差十分就十一點；現在是十點

           五十分。   movie〔ˈmuvɪ〕*n.* 電影

           without〔wɪðˈaut〕*prep.* 沒有

           either〔ˈiðɚ〕*adj.*（兩者之中）任一的

For question number 7, please look at picture E.

7. (**A**) Which balloon is the highest?
      A. The one with stars.
      B. The lightest one.
      C. The one with three children on it.

    * balloon〔bəˈlun〕n. 氣球　　star〔stɑr〕n. 星狀物
      light〔laɪt〕adj. 輕的

For question number 8, please look at picture F.

8. (**A**) Who will help the people in the building?
      A. Firefighters will help them.
      B. They are shouting and waving.
      C. There are four people in the building.

    * building〔ˈbɪldɪŋ〕n. 建築物
      firefighter〔ˈfaɪrˌfaɪtɚ〕n. 消防隊員
      shout〔ʃaʊt〕v. 喊叫　　wave〔wev〕v. 揮手

For question number 9, please look at picture G.

9. (**A**) How many times have they jumped rope?
      A. They have jumped twice so far.
      B. They count while they jump rope.
      C. There are three children jumping rope.

    * *How many~?*　~多少?　　time〔taɪm〕n. 次數
      jump〔dʒʌmp〕v. 跳　　rope〔rop〕n. 繩子
      jump rope 跳繩　　twice〔twaɪs〕adv. 兩次
      so far 到目前爲止　　count〔kaʊnt〕v. 數
      while〔hwaɪl〕conj. 當…的時候

For question number 10, please look at picture H.

10. (**B**) How is she holding the rabbits?

    A. She is holding two rabbits.

    B. She is holding them carefully.

    C. One white one and one black one.

    * hold〔hold〕v. 抱著   rabbit〔'ræbɪt〕n. 兔子

       carefully〔'kɛrfəlɪ〕adv. 小心地

第二部份

11. (**C**) Is this your jacket?

    A. It's beautiful.

    B. You didn't have to bring a gift!

    C. Thank you. I must have dropped it.

    * jacket〔'dʒækɪt〕n. 夾克

      beautiful〔'bjutəfəl〕adj. 漂亮的   gift〔gɪft〕n. 禮物

      must have* + *p.p. 當時一定（表示對過去的肯定推測）

      drop〔drɑp〕v. 掉落

12. (**B**) Which page is the diagram on?

    A. Chapter three.

    B. Ninety-seven.

    C. In the textbook.

    * page〔pedʒ〕n.（書等的）頁

      diagram〔'daɪə,græm〕n. 圖表

      chapter〔'tʃæptɚ〕n.（書的）章

      textbook〔'tɛkst,buk〕n. 教科書

13. (**B**) How much ice cream do you want?

    A. I'd like chocolate, please.

    B. Two scoops, please.

    C. It's fifty dollars.

    * ***ice cream*** 冰淇淋　　***would like*** 想要 (＝ *want*)
      chocolate〔'tʃɔkəlɪt〕*n.* 巧克力
      scoop〔skup〕*n.* (一)杓

14. (**C**) Do you know what time this train arrives at Keelung?

    A. Yes.

    B. Yes, it's going to Keelung.

    C. About six o'clock.

    * arrive〔ə'raɪv〕*v.* 抵達　　***Keelung*** 基隆

15. (**A**) Give me a call when you are free.

    A. I'll do that.

    B. I'll give it to you when I'm finished with it.

    C. Here you are.

    * ***give*** *sb.* ***a call*** 打電話給某人
      free〔fri〕*adj.* 有空的　　finished〔'fɪnɪʃt〕*adj.* 完成的
      Here you are. 你要的東西在這裡；拿去吧。(＝ *Here it is.*)

16. (**A**) Will you be finished with this book by tonight?

    A. I think so.　　　　B. I will buy it later.

    C. Yes, I can.

    * by〔baɪ〕*prep.* 在…之前　　tonight〔tə'naɪt〕*adv.* 今晚
      later〔'letɚ〕*adv.* 稍後；以後

17. (**C**) Spring is in the air today!

    A. Yes, I see it over there.

    B. You had better close the window.

    C. Yes, it's a lovely day.

    * spring〔sprɪŋ〕*n.* 春天　　air〔ɛr〕*n.* 空氣
      in the air 在空中　　***over there*** 在那裡
      had better + 原形動詞　最好　　close〔kloz〕*v.* 關上
      window〔'wɪndo〕*n.* 窗戶　　lovely〔'lʌvlɪ〕*adj.* 可愛的

18. (**A**) Did you enjoy the show?

    A. I thought the paintings were wonderful.

    B. They are a little too tight.

    C. It's on the second floor.

    * enjoy〔ɪn'dʒɔɪ〕*v.* 喜歡　　show〔ʃo〕*n.* 展覽
      painting〔'pentɪŋ〕*n.* 繪畫
      wonderful〔'wʌndɚfəl〕*adj.* 很棒的　　***a little*** 有一點
      tight〔taɪt〕*adj.* 緊的　　floor〔flor〕*n.* 樓層

19. (**B**) Let me give you a hand with that.

    A. Nice to meet you, too.

    B. You're too kind.

    C. Your performance was wonderful.

    * let〔lɛt〕*v.* 讓　　***give sb. a hand*** 幫助某人 < *with* >
      Nice to meet you, too. 我也很高興能認識你。
      kind〔kaɪnd〕*adj.* 好心的
      performance〔pɚ'fɔrməns〕*n.* 表演

20. (**B**) Weren't you going to go swimming today?

     A. No, you weren't.

     B. Yes, but the pool is closed.

     C. Yes, I'd love to go swimming.

     * **go swimming** 去游泳   pool〔pul〕*n.* 游泳池

       closed〔klozd〕*adj.* 關閉的

       would love to V. 想要（= *would like to V.*）

第三部份

21. (**C**) M: What time does the movie start?

     W: There is a show at 6:00 and another one at 7:30.

     M: You mean you haven't bought the tickets yet? What if both shows are sold out?

     W: Then we'll just go to another one.

     Question : What will they do if they cannot buy tickets to the movie?

     A. They will go another day.

     B. They will do something else.

     C. They will see a different movie.

     * start〔stɑrt〕*v.* 開始   show〔ʃo〕*n.* 電影播放

       mean〔min〕*v.* 意思是   ticket〔'tɪkɪt〕*n.* 入場券

       yet〔jɛt〕*adv.* 還（沒）   **What if…?** 如果…該怎麼辦？

       sell out 賣光   then〔ðɛn〕*adv.* 那麼

       different〔'dɪfərənt〕*adj.* 不同的；另外的

22. (**B**)　M：What did you say?　I can hardly hear you.

W：Is this any better?

M：A little.　Try to speak up.

Question：Why can't the man understand the woman?

A. She does not speak clearly.

B. She speaks too softly.

C. She does not understand English well.

* hardly〔'hardlɪ〕 *adv.* 幾乎不
hear〔hɪr〕 *v.* 聽見　　*speak up* 更大聲地說
understand〔,ʌndɚ'stænd〕 *v.* 了解
clearly〔'klɪrlɪ〕 *adv.* 清楚地　softly〔'sɔftlɪ〕 *adv.* 輕聲地
well〔wɛl〕 *adv.* 充分地；十分地

23. (**B**)　W：Have you heard about Jerry?

M：No.　What happened?

W：He was admitted to NTU.

M：That's great.　I hope I am as lucky.

Question：What does the man mean?

A. He hopes to win the lottery.

B. He hopes to go to NTU.

C. He hopes Jerry is lucky at NTU.

* ***hear about*** 得知關於…的消息
happen〔'hæpən〕 *v.* 發生
admit〔əd'mɪt〕 *v.* 准許進入 < *to* >
NTU 國立台灣大學 (= *National Taiwan University*)
great〔gret〕 *adj.* 很棒的　　hope〔hop〕 *v.* 希望
as〔æz〕 *adv.* 跟…一樣地　　lucky〔'lʌkɪ〕 *adj.* 幸運的
win〔wɪn〕 *v.* 贏得　　lottery〔'latərɪ〕 *n.* 彩券；樂透

24. (**C**) M : Thank you for coming in.

        W : It was my pleasure. When do you think you will choose someone for the job?

        M : We will make our decision by the end of the week.

        W : Well, I hope to hear good news then.

        Question : What will happen to the woman by the end of the week?

        A. She will choose the job.

        B. She will hear some good news.

        C. She will know whether she got the job.

     * ***come in*** 進來   pleasure〔'plɛʒɚ〕*n.* 榮幸

       choose〔tʃuz〕*v.* 選擇   job〔dʒɑb〕*n.* 工作

       decision〔dɪ'sɪʒən〕*n.* 決定   end〔ɛnd〕*n.* 結束；末尾

       news〔njuz〕*n.* 消息   then〔ðɛn〕*adv.* 那時

       sth. ***happen to*** *sb.* 某人發生某事

       whether〔'hwɛðɚ〕*conj.* 是否

25. (**B**) M : Why was Martin late for school today?

        W : He said that he missed the bus.

        M : But he walks to school!

        W : Then he was just making an excuse.

        Question : Why was Martin late for school?

       A. He walked too slowly.   B. We don't know.

       C. He missed the bus.

     * late〔let〕*adj.* 遲到的   miss〔mɪs〕*v.* 錯過

       excuse〔ɪk'skjus〕*n.* 理由；藉口

       slowly〔'slolɪ〕*adv.* 緩慢地

26. (**C**) W: It's supposed to rain heavily so you had better take your umbrella.

M: Where did you hear that?

W: On the radio.

M: Oh, those weather forecasters always get it wrong.

Question : What does the man think about the weather forecast for today?

A. He thinks it will probably rain.

B. He thinks it would be wrong not to take an umbrella.

C. He thinks it is probably wrong.

* suppose〔sə'poz〕*v.* 猜想　　*be supposed to V.* 應該
  heavily〔'hɛvɪlɪ〕*adv.* 猛烈地　　*rain heavily* 下大雨
  umbrella〔ʌm'brɛlə〕*n.* 雨傘　　radio〔'redɪ,o〕*n.* 廣播
  forecaster〔for'kæstɚ〕*n.* 預測者
  weather forecaster 天氣預報員
  wrong〔rɔŋ〕*adj.* 錯誤的　　*get it wrong* 誤解；算錯
  think about 認為　　forecast〔'for,kæst〕*n.* 預測
  weather forecast 天氣預報
  probably〔'prɑbəblɪ〕*adv.* 可能

27. (**A**) M: Have you decided?

W: Yes. I'll have the chicken.

M: Fries or rice with that?

W: Rice, please. And I'd also like to order a salad.

Question : What comes with the chicken?

A. A choice of French fries or rice.

B. Rice and a salad.

C. Rice, and French fries or a salad.

* decide〔dɪˈsaɪd〕v. 決定　　have〔hæv〕v. 吃
  chicken〔ˈtʃɪkən〕n. 雞肉
  fries〔fraɪz〕n. pl. 薯條（= French fries）
  rice〔raɪs〕n. 米飯　　salad〔ˈsæləd〕n. 沙拉
  come with 與～一同供應　　choice〔tʃɔɪs〕n. 選擇

28. (**A**) W: To prepare for tomorrow's test, study chapter seven.

　　　 M: Will the new formulas be on the test?

　　　 W: Anything that is chapter seven might be on the test.

　　　 M: So I guess we should read the whole chapter.

Question : What does the teacher tell the students?

A. Something that is in chapter seven might be
    on the test.

B. The new formulas will not be on the test.

C. The new formulas can be found in chapter eight.

* prepare〔prɪˈpɛr〕v. 準備　　test〔tɛst〕n. 考試
  study〔ˈstʌdɪ〕v. 研讀
  formula〔ˈfɔrmjələ〕n. 公式
  guess〔gɛs〕v. 猜想　　whole〔hol〕adj. 全部的；整個的

29. (**C**) W: Who are you rooting for?

M: Oh, I hope the Dragons win.

W: Are they your favorite team?

M: No, but I like them better than the Lions.

Question : Why does the man want the Dragons to win?

A. He is a big Dragons fan.

B. The Lions are not playing today.

C. He prefers them to the Lions.

* root〔rut〕v. 加油　　***root for*** 為…加油
dragon〔'drægən〕n. 龍　　win〔wɪn〕v. 贏
favorite〔'fevərɪt〕adj. 最喜愛的　　team〔tim〕n. 隊伍
like~better 更喜歡~　　lion〔'laɪən〕n. 獅子
fan〔fæn〕n.（球）迷　　prefer〔prɪ'fɝ〕v. 比較喜歡
prefer A ***to*** B 喜歡 A 勝過 B

30. (**B**) W: How was the math test?

M: I thought it was pretty easy, but John said it
was hard.

W: Why?

M: I don't know.　Maybe he didn't study hard enough.

Question : What did John say about the math test?

A. He said he didn't study enough.

B. He said it was too hard.

C. He said it was pretty easy.

* math〔mæθ〕n. 數學　　pretty〔'prɪtɪ〕adv. 相當
hard〔hɑrd〕adj. 困難的　　maybe〔'mebɪ〕adv. 或許

附錄

全民英語能力分級檢定測驗簡介

　　「全民英語能力分級檢定測驗」（General English Proficiency Test），簡稱「全民英檢」（GEPT），旨在提供我國各階段英語學習者一公平、可靠、具效度之英語能力評量工具，測驗對象包括在校學生及一般社會人士，可做為學習成果檢定、教學改進及公民營機構甄選人才等之參考。

　　本測驗為標準參照測驗（criterion-referenced test），參考當前我國英語教育體制，制定分級標準，整套系統共分五級——初級（Elementary）、中級（Intermediate）、中高級（High-Intermediate）、高級（Advanced）、優級（Superior）。每級訂有明確能力標準（詳見表一綜合能力說明），報考者可依英語能力選擇適當級數報考，每級均包含聽、說、讀、寫四項完整的測驗，通過所報考級數的能力標準即可取得該級的合格證書。各級命題設計均參考目前各階段英語教育之課程大綱及相關教材之內容分析，期能符合國內各階段英語教育的需求、反應本土的生活經驗與特色。

「全民英語能力檢定分級測驗」各級綜合能力說明　　《表一》

級數	綜　合　能　力	備　　　　註	
初級	通過初級測驗者具有基礎英語能力，能理解和使用淺易日常用語，英語能力相當於國中畢業者。	建議下列人員宜具有該級英語能力	一般行政助理、維修技術人員、百貨業、餐飲業、旅館業或觀光景點服務人員、計程車駕駛等。
中級	通過中級測驗者具有使用簡單英語進行日常生活溝通的能力，英語能力相當於高中職畢業者。		一般行政、業務、技術、銷售人員、護理人員、旅館、飯店接待人員、總機人員、警政人員、旅遊從業人員等。
中高級	通過中高級測驗者英語能力逐漸成熟，應用的領域擴大，雖有錯誤，但無礙溝通，英語能力相當於大學非英語主修系所畢業者。		商務、企劃人員、祕書、工程師、研究助理、空服人員、航空機師、航管人員、海關人員、導遊、外事警政人員、新聞從業人員、資訊管理人員等。

級數	綜　合　能　力		備　　註
高級	通過高級測驗者英語流利順暢，僅有少許錯誤，應用能力擴及學術或專業領域，英語能力相當於國內大學英語主修系所或曾赴英語系國家大學或研究所進修並取得學位者。	建議下列人員宜具有該級英語能力	高級商務人員、協商談判人員、英語教學人員、研究人員、翻譯人員、外交人員、國際新聞從業人員等。
優級	通過優級測驗者的英語能力接近受過高等教育之母語人士，各種場合均能使用適當策略作最有效的溝通。		專業翻譯人員、國際新聞特派人員、外交官員、協商談判主談人員等。

初級英語能力測驗簡介

I. 通過初級檢定者的英語能力

聽	説	讀	寫
能聽懂簡易的英語句子、對話及故事。	能簡單地自我介紹並以簡易英語對答；能朗讀簡易文章。	能瞭解簡易英語對話、短文、故事及書信的內容；能看懂常用的標示。	能寫簡單的英語句子及段落。

II. 測 驗 內 容

	初　試			複　試
測驗項目	聽力測驗	閱讀能力測驗	寫作能力測驗	口説能力測驗
總題數	30	35	16	18
作答時間／分鐘	約 20	35	40	約 10
測驗內容	看圖辨義 問答 簡短對話	詞彙和結構 段落填空 閱讀理解	單句寫作 段落寫作	複誦 朗讀句子與短文 回答問題

　　聽力及閱讀能力測驗成績採標準計分方式，60分為平均數，滿分120分。寫作及口說能力測驗成績採整體式評分，使用級分制，分為0～5級分，再轉換成百分制。各項成績通過標準如下：

III. 成績計算及通過標準

初　試	通過標準／滿分	複　試	通過標準／滿分
聽力測驗 閱讀能力測驗 寫作能力測驗	80／120分 80／120分 70／100分	口說能力測驗	80／100分

IV. 寫作能力測驗級分說明

第一部份：單句寫作級分說明

級　分	說　　明
2	正確無誤。
1	有誤，但重點結構正確。
0	錯誤過多、未答、等同未答。

第二部份：段落寫作級分說明

級　分	說　　明
5	正確表達題目之要求；文法、用字等幾乎無誤。
4	大致正確表達題目之要求；文法、用字等有誤，但不影響讀者之理解。
3	大致回答題目之要求，但未能完全達意；文法、用字等有誤，稍影響讀者之理解。
2	部份回答題目之要求，表達上有令人不解／誤解之處；文法、用字等皆有誤，讀者須耐心解讀。
1	僅回答1個問題或重點；文法、用字等錯誤過多，嚴重影響讀者之理解。
0	未答、等同未答。

各部份題型之題數、級分及總分計算公式：

分項測驗	測驗題型	各部份題數	每題級分	佔總分比重
第一部份：單句寫作	A. 句子改寫	5題	2分	50 %
	B. 句子合併	5題	2分	
	C. 重組	5題	2分	
第二部份：段落寫作	看圖表寫作	1篇	5分	50 %
總分計算公式	公式：{(第一部份得分/30)＋(第二部份得分/5)}×50 例：第一部份各項得分 A－8分 　　　　　　　　　　　　B－10分 　　　　　　　　　　　　C－8分 8+10+8=26 三項加總第一部份得分 — 26分 第二部份得分 — 4分 依公式計算如下： {(26/30)＋(4/5)}×50=83　該考生得分83分			

　　凡應考且合乎規定者一律發給成績單。初試及複試各項測驗成績通過者，發給合格證書，本測驗成績紀錄保存兩年。

　　初試通過者，可於一年內單獨報考複試，得重複報考。惟複試一旦通過，即不得再報考。

　　已通過本英檢測驗初級，一年內不得再報考同級數之測驗。違反本規定報考者，其應試資格將被取消，且不退費。

（以上資料取自「全民英檢學習網站」http://www.gept.org.tw）

劉毅英文「八年級第一次英文單字大賽」
前 100 名得獎同學名單

名次	姓 名	學 校	班級	名次	姓 名	學 校	班級	名次	姓 名	學 校	班級
1	呂馥伊	弘道國中	807	35	陳乙斯	建成國中	803	69	駱昱安	江翠國中	824
2	楊雅筑	北安國中	808	36	陳怡安	芳和國中	801	70	邱柏綸	北安國中	812
3	林 朗	光仁中學	8孝	37	陳睿怡	士林國中	804	71	黃郁晴	興雅國中	715
4	沈玉歆	南門國中	813	38	林怡伶	興福國中	805	72	黃新儒	新莊國中	841
5	史宜平	江翠國中	816	39	林瑞怡	大直國中	809	73	張 尹	木柵國中	801
6	黃威棣	實踐國中	801	40	邱品瑄	景興國中	718	74	孟純德	建成國中	811
7	林之嵐	長安國中	807	41	王子翎	大同中學	802	75	蔡翊琳	懷生國中	803
8	徐若瑄	重慶國中	819	42	蕭丞晏	福和國中	711	76	謝佳霖	建成國中	810
9	徐智威	江翠國中	815	43	李 惟	實踐國中	802	77	林欣儀	金華國中	813
10	林 嬙	士林國中	817	44	李冠瑩	忠孝國中	804	78	林厚樑	建成國中	811
11	李宇倫	古亭國小	604	45	鄭儒聰	建成國中	803	79	陳柄錡	積穗國中	714
12	賴又嘉	新民國中	707	46	許珮華	建成國中	811	80	羅思寧	師大附中	154
13	林語軒	天母國中	817	47	王姿雅	石牌國中	714	81	韋伯函	大同中學	806
14	駱子皓	聖心國小	4B	48	呂學漢	長安國中	809	82	張子欣	鄧公國小	505
15	蘇容萱	萬華國中	820	49	丘碩元	福和國中	724	83	巫哲嘉	古亭國中	807
16	張婷雅	江翠國中	816	50	曹郁雯	建成國中	803	84	斯 婕	士林國中	804
17	黃柏鈞	江翠國中	816	51	謝岳宏	建成國中	810	85	周貞言	師大附中	151
18	黃子娟	延平中學	803	52	蘇冠霖	樹林國中	820	86	吳欣儒	仁愛國中	817
19	楊博丞	竹林國中	8勤	53	位宇勳	萬華國中	723	87	林淳淳	忠孝國中	802
20	劉易青	江翠國中	816	54	許誌珍	士林國中	816	88	張筵婕	大安國中	813
21	張恆律	金華國中	816	55	鄧顯娟	北安國中	809	89	吳典安	大安國中	817
22	劉憶璇	大直國中	803	56	蘇郁雯	萬華國中	808	90	蔡 寧	天母國中	803
23	孫伊蓮	敦化國小	507	57	吳岱軒	中正國中	707	91	葉芃筠	師大附中	154
24	沈若函	慈文國中	805	58	劉柏廷	敦化國中	821	92	林彥辰	江翠國中	816
25	王詠萱	大安國中	804	59	林佳錦	忠孝國中	810	93	孫語霙	萬華國中	817
26	林韋辰	大直國中	802	60	許雅婷	中崙國中	805	94	鄭凱文	健康國小	605
27	陳佑任	敦化國中	819	61	邱睿涵	介壽國中	802	95	陳佩琪	大安國中	807
28	林羿萱	重慶國中	704	62	馬浩屏	石牌國中	806	96	張書蓉	重慶國中	815
29	黃詩穎	敦化國中	703	63	原 薇	建安國小	516	97	蔡佳民	金陵女中	803
30	曹尚敏	士林國中	804	64	方詠萱	中正國中	811	98	陳元亨	建成國中	703
31	蔡若涵	士林國中	812	65	謝岳彤	建成國中	708	99	李偉愷	中山國中	809
32	李瑞娟	薇閣國中	8平	66	劉擇淵	長安國中	801	100	連庭璇	敦化國中	714
33	賴文平	景興國中	815	67	廖晟宇	蘭雅國中	701				
34	徐 冬	興福國中	805	68	詹盈盈	萬華國中	714				

劉毅英文家教班國一班成績優異同學名單

姓名	學校	分數	姓名	學校	分數	姓名	學校	分數	姓名	學校	分數
張家偉	復興國中	94	姚永珍	市中正國中	82	蕭韋柏	百齡國中	73	陳美好	仁愛國中	68
陳彥伶	溪崑國中	93	江勻楷	金華國中	82	郭旭程	景興國中	73	王玠璉	重慶國中	68
黃葳琳	金華國小	92	涂黛	師大附中	82	陳彥良	辭修中學	73	阮柏凱	溪崑國中	6
向峻毅	金華國中	91	薛怡冠	敦化國中	81	劉冠廷	福和國中	73	林庭安	敦化國中	68
邱鈺婷	仁愛國中	90	吳育瑄	集美國小	81	林俊達	楊明國小	73	王子豪	秀峰國中	6
嚴唯寧	麗山國小	90	李采凌	市中正國中	81	黃奕棣	蘭雅國中	73	王珩聿	五峰國中	6
陳青妤	介壽國中	90	蔡沅劭	忠孝國中	80	姜俊羽	信義國中	73	劉旃甯	弘道國中	6
張碩庭	石牌國小	90	周鈺倩	萬華國中	80	吳則緯	內湖國小	73	李翊華	明志國中	6
陳詩昀	福和國中	90	陳宛愉	三民國中	79	鄭懿	南門國中	72	王筱萱	仁愛國中	6
李冠瑩	明志國中	89	唐鈺婷	福和國中	79	林芷予	重慶國中	72	劉益蓉	師大附中	6
鄭皓云	新莊國中	89	于荃	古亭國小	79	蕭文莉	仁愛國中	72	吳秉諭	景興國中	6
陳盈臻	溪崑國中	89	沈羿文	仁愛國中	79	金皓鈞	東山中學	72	黃毓雯	秀峰國中	6
杜佳勳	金陵女中	89	簡愷均	文化國小	79	何宇屏	石門國中	72	吳貞燁	長安國中	6
羅予平	興雅國中	89	陳柏修	三重國中	79	林意馨	市中正國中	72	張家林	弘道國中	6
王安佳	蘆洲國中	89	陳曉璇	金華國中	78	洪逸寧	萬芳國中	72	伊晟	天母國中	6
李元甫	銘傳國中	88	鄭凱文	健康國小	78	馬韻婷	懷生國中	72	江奕璇	懷生國中	6
王俊升	重慶國小	87	馬唯庭	衛理女中	78	周育德	再興中學	71	黃韋晴	衛理女中	6
藍紫与	市中正國中	87	許家弘	金華國中	78	簡翔凌	古亭國小	71	王公勻	弘道國中	6
任蕭東	立人中學	87	徐偉傑	大同中學	78	陳澈	大安國中	71	丁乃群	醒吾中學	6
白善尹	敦化國小	87	邱韋豪	溪崑國中	77	宋睿予	景興國中	71	巫逸慈	鷺江國小	6
林唯中	北政國中	86	盛筠	南門國中	77	謝喬安	二信中學	71	林家安	三和國中	6
陳芷琳	福和國中	86	賴梵于	光仁中學	77	游雅婷	中山國中	70	李麒萱	明志國中	6
劉彥翎	介壽國中	86	邱耀賢	格致中學	77	謝承芳	大安國中	70	吳冠宏	重慶國小	6
吳佩熹	金華國中	86	邱聿韶	仁愛國中	76	蔡甯安	新莊國中	70	曾子涵	新莊國中	6
胡格瑄	萬芳國中	86	黃彥愷	敦化國小	76	張峻毓	大安國中	70	洪聖傑	市中正國中	6
陳齊	市中正國中	86	王尹廷	百齡國中	76	陳逸宏	再興中學	70	吳欣蕙	恆毅中學	6
游秉憲	弘道國中	86	楊亞曼	百齡國中	76	顏孟鐸	南湖國小	70	劉冠儀	新莊國中	6
孫克瑀	景興國中	85	周育玄	萬華國中	76	李治毅	日新國小	70	謝富竹	忠孝國中	6
黃韻蓉	薇閣國小	85	曾尹澍	瑠公國中	76	魏伯州	辛亥國小	70	李元夫	弘道國中	6
藍德新	秀朗國小	85	鄭宇婷	延平中學	76	陳宣翰	三和國中	70	單甯	信義國中	6
張詩怡	重慶國小	84	陳曄	內湖國中	76	林書丞	市中正國中	69	林品慧	秀峰國中	6
賈其蓁	新莊國中	84	高昕妤	石牌國中	75	陳禹廷	仁愛國中	69	陳孟君	中山國中	6
賴映儒	介壽國中	84	呂學宸	興雅國中	75	許采玲	大安國中	69	鄭家欣	廣福國中	6
楊子賢	龍門國中	84	張堯	大直國中	75	郭恬馨	金華國中	69	黃信和	金華國中	6
連品涵	大安國中	84	張博彥	東新國中	75	林政毅	集美國小	69	楊挺笙	延平中學	6
楊書瑋	北安國中	84	陳赴妤	靜心國中	75	楊耕毅	新生國中	69	呂依臻	薇閣國中	6
許顥今	麗山國中	84	蔣永軒	東門國小	75	陳志愷	金華國中	69	林觀宇	市中正國中	6
郭安哲	修德國小	83	劉佩怡	聖心中學	75	洪珮瓊	光仁中學	69	蘇郁涵	萬大國小	6
駱冠廷	懷生國中	83	倪靖宗	二信中學	74	林士群	復興國中	69	謝畢宇	碧華國中	6
任鎔宜	立人中學	83	張書倫	懷生國中	74	許博凱	重慶國中	68	王公喬	弘道國中	6
王楚薇	中山國中	83	梁崇柏	景興國中	74	林璨德	信義國小	68			
彭世安	國北師實小	82	朱敬仁	再興中學	74	楊惠勤	三和國中	68			

劉毅英文家教班國二班成績優異同學名單

姓名	學校	分數	姓名	學校	分數	姓名	學校	分數	姓名	學校	分數
許民豪	建成國中	100	黃沛嘉	金華國中	93	馬瑞梅	鷺江國中	89	潘盈臻	弘道國中	86
何穎志	延平中學	100	洪會洋	麗山國中	93	孫沛瑜	金華國中	89	莫斯宇	永和國中	86
劉庭妤	敦化國小	98	蔣永涵	古亭國中	93	陳奕翔	三和國中	89	王欣寧	崇光國中	86
林書含	延平中學	98	郭冠呈	延平中學	93	曾淳嘉	弘道國中	89	江勁緯	新莊國中	86
陳鵬宇	新莊國中	98	黃彥瑄	敦化國中	93	蔡寧	天母國中	89	張筳婕	大安國中	86
劉憶璇	大直國中	98	李沆哲	海山中學	93	林一先	金華國中	89	郭景源	士林國中	86
吳昕儒	金華國中	97	李勁毅	萬華國中	93	王靖雯	重慶國中	88	劉羿廷	興雅國中	86
張庭慈	介壽國中	97	孟純德	建成國中	92	游爾欣	市中正國中	88	蔡佩如	竹林國中	85
陳緯倫	格致中學	97	鄭晏羽	格致中學	92	江志浩	三重國中	88	黃薇名	三重國中	85
陳奕萱	延平中學	96	蔡文馨	中崙國中	92	李治昕	新埔國中	88	張雅甄	木柵國中	85
黃振剛	延平中學	96	盧禹瑄	金華國中	92	胡芝嘉	市中正國中	88	詹前聖	大直國中	85
吳岱軒	市中正國中	96	林姿伶	弘道國中	92	許瑋庭	新莊國中	88	劉瀚元	新莊國中	85
陳柏翰	延平中學	96	鄭學鴻	延平中學	92	陳怡安	復興國中	88	呂哲旻	新莊國小	85
陳博雄	中山國中	96	楊佳穎	敦化國中	92	徐子婷	金陵女中	88	陳威宏	縣立中正國中	85
陳祖慧	崇光國中	96	連庭璇	敦化國中	92	徐泓楷	弘道國中	88	廖晟宇	蘭雅國中	84
陳家安	瑠公國中	96	修偉翔	長安國中	92	魏敏琦	大直國中	88	楊瑞祁	新興國中	84
陳里仁	萬華國中	96	林欣儀	金華國中	92	黃執中	介壽國中	88	陳麒中	百齡國中	84
陳誌珍	士林國中	96	王詠萱	大安國中	92	施怡靜	大安國中	88	姜怡廷	金陵女中	84
陳頒	麗山國中	96	巢瑞麟	秀峰國中	92	鄭敬翰	延平中學	88	楊馥嘉	士林國中	84
陳子娟	延平中學	96	劉珈予	仁愛國小	92	劉穎恩	敦化國中	88	曾台安	薇閣國中	84
陳瑞怡	大直國中	96	廖常至	永和國中	92	賴一銘	格致中學	88	邱柏綸	北安國中	84
陳俊儀	光仁中學	96	賴玟秀	西松國中	92	王新惠	長安國中	88	謝秉蓁	永和國中	84
陳承霈	光仁中學	96	許書衡	東山中學	92	陳一慧	金華國中	88	黃琬淳	興雅國中	84
陳鈺淵	新莊國中	96	沈若函	慈文國中	92	陳毅鴻	敦化國中	88	陳麗宇	金華國中	84
陳思樺	敦化國中	95	陳韻晴	醒吾中學	92	徐億恩	新莊國中	87	簡竹均	南門國中	84
陳玉歆	南門國中	95	李均儀	麗山中學	92	蘇冠霖	樹林國中	87	林欣諺	再興中學	84
陳貞言	師大附中	94	黃建勳	再興中學		鄭任傑	延平中學	87	曹佳琪	成德國中	84
陳慧暄	光仁中學	94	張智陞	永和國中		利采穎	江翠國中	87	李佳昱	五峰國中	84
陳盈瑋	市中正國中	94	吳駿碁	秀峰國中	91	賴昱帆	崇光國中	87	吳本立	師大附中	84
陳永達	建成國中	94	湯博鈞	福和國中	91	蔡家軒	懷生國中	87	姚若凡	竹林國中	84
陳姿雅	石牌國中	94	林育勳	時雨國中	90	莊鑫奇	溪崑國中	86	林怡慧	新莊國中	84
陳郁雯	萬華國中	94	林憶如	新埔國中	90	吳筱珊	敦化國中	86	連宥甄	達人國中	84
陳瑋萱	延平中學	94	朱敬文	再興中學	90	林思岑	長安國中	86	林姍吟	介壽國中	84
陳文懷	中崙國中	94	吳柏諺	明志國中	90	徐嬿鴻	金華國中	86	黃柏鈞	興雅國中	84
陳繼宥	文山國中	94	胡哲輔	徐匯國中	90	黃啓銘	新莊國中	86	呂依瑾	薇閣國中	84
陳佩琪	大安國中	94	林宛廷	景美國中	90	吳典安	大安國中	86	呂禕芸	華興國中	84
陳佳穎	復興國小	94	康晉寧	弘道國中	90	李怡靜	中崙國中	86	林珈妃	忠孝國中	84
陳勁甫	深坑國中	94	蕭丞晏	福和國中	90	王奕婷	金陵女中	86	袁國智	中山國中	84
陳偉愷	中山國中	94	蘇俊瑋	市中正國中	90	魏啓翰	仁愛國中	86	鄒沛哲	介壽國中	84
陳協勳	延平中學	94	黃孺雅	三民國中	90	劉宜庭	積穗國中	86			
陳柏廷	敦化國中	93	陳柏廷	光仁中學	89	蔡明諺	長安國中	86			
陳章平	敦化國中	93	章庭瑋	明志國中	89	洪芫萱	南門國中	86			

|||||||||||||| ● 學習出版公司門市部 ● ||||||||||||||

台北地區：台北市許昌街 10 號 2 樓 TEL：(02)2331-4060・2331-9209
台中地區：台中市綠川東街 32 號 8 樓 23 室
　　　　　TEL：(04)2223-2838

||||||||||||||||||||||||||||||||||||||||||||||||

初級英語聽力檢定④

主　　　編／劉　毅
發　行　所／學習出版有限公司　　　　☎ (02) 2704-5525
郵 撥 帳 號／0512727-2 學習出版社帳戶
登　記　證／局版台業 2179 號
印　刷　所／裕強彩色印刷有限公司
台 北 門 市／台北市許昌街 10 號 2 F　　　☎ (02) 2331-4060・2331-9209
台 中 門 市／台中市綠川東街 32 號 8 F 23 室　　☎ (04) 2223-2838
台灣總經銷／紅螞蟻圖書有限公司　　　☎ (02) 2799-9490・2657-0132
美國總經銷／Evergreen Book Store　　☎ (818) 2813622

售價：新台幣一百八十元正
2005 年 1 月 1 日初版

ISBN 957-519-810-7